A Lady in the Sheets, A Savage in the Streets

Andrea

A Lady in the Sheets, A Savage in the Streets

Copyright © 2017 by Andrea

www.shanpresents.com

This book is a work of fiction. Names, characters, places, and incidents either are the product of the author's imagination or are used fictitiously and are not to be construed as real. Any resemblance to actual persons, living or dead, business establishments, events, or locales or, is entirely coincidental.

No portion of this book may be used or reproduced in any manner whatsoever without writer permission except in the case of brief quotations embodied in critical articles and reviews.

Text Shan to 22828 to stay up to date with new releases, sneak peeks, contest, and more...

Check your spam if you don't receive an email thanking you for signing up.

Text SPROMANCE to 22828 to stay up to date on new releases, plus get information on contest, sneak peeks, and more!

Table of Contents

Chapter 1: Miyonna Pierce 1

Chapter 2: Juelz Johnson..10

Chapter 3: Monte Washington 23

Chapter 4: Ameerah Statum...31

Chapter 5: Miyonna Pierce 41

Chapter 6: Juelz Johnson...53

Chapter 7: Ameerah Statum...70

Chapter 8: Monte Washington 85

Chapter 9: Juelz Johnson...97

Chapter 10: Miyonna Pierce- Johnson 114

Chapter 11: Ameerah Statum 127

Chapter 12: Juelz Johnson..140

Chapter 13: Monte Washington 149

Chapter 14: Miyonna Pierce- Johnson 171

Chapter 15: Juelz Johnson..185

Chapter 16: Tiyonna Pierce 204

Chapter 17: Miyonna Pierce- Johnson 210

Chapter 18: Juelz Johnson..223

Chapter 1: Miyonna Pierce

Bang! Bang! Bang!

I let my Desert Eagle do the talking, as I emptied the clip into my target's skull. He was a nigga that owed me some money, and I was very playful and liked to laugh and joke around, but one thing I didn't play about was my money. I was a boss in every aspect of the word, so I carried business how it should be carried. I acquired a whole empire in the streets, which my father passed down to me before he died. I was the oldest kid so I got the empire, and I worked extra hard to keep things the way that he had left them. I upgraded slightly, but that was it. All the workers respected me, and that was how it was supposed to be.

Wait, before I go any further, let me introduce myself to y'all. My name is Miyona. I'm a 28-year-old mix breed. I'm mixed with Black, Indian, and Mexican. My mother is Mexican and my father is Black and Indian. I guess my dad liked a little swirl with his coffee.

Standing at five foot five, I was two hundred and ten pounds. Yup, I was a thick 'ems, but I was good with my shit meaning that I took good care of my body. I waist-trained a lot to keep my stomach in check, but my thighs were thick and juicy just like my nigga liked them. My ass was nice, too. I wasn't bragging, but extra thick bitches were definitely winning out here.

Andrea

Anyway, I have two kids and a fiancé. He knows what I do and he respects it. Being in the game is actually how I met him. Juelz used to cop work from my father. One day, I walked into the meeting because I needed to talk to my dad, and he was staring hard as hell at me. I couldn't lie and say that I wasn't impressed with what I saw, either, because I was.

He was standing there fine as hell. Dreads looking like they were freshly twisted, and I loved that shit. I had a thing for dread heads. Not the ones that hang low, but the ones that are shoulder-length. He had on jeans that sagged slightly and a short-sleeve, V-neck t-shirt that showed off his muscles. He stood at six foot one, and I could tell through his shirt that he had a rock-hard body. By the way he was standing, I knew he was packing something serious, too.

I walked out the room to wait for the meeting to be over, and when it was, Juelz came out like he was looking for me. When he spotted me, he walked towards me and started to talk to me. I had so much confidence in myself that I asked him out. From the first night we went out, we were inseparable, but we kept a relationship that soon blossomed on the low. Well, that was until I ended up pregnant. I had to go and tell my dad. He wasn't happy at first, but by the end of my pregnancy, he came around and excepted our relationship. I guess he saw how happy Juelz made me. That was almost six years ago, and we were still hanging on and holding in there. Our love got stronger each day.

A Lady in the Sheets, A Savage in the Streets

I kept my dealings in the streets away from my home life. Juelz did, too. We knew that, once we walked through the doors of our home, it was about our family. In the streets, people called me Poca. Everyone joked about me looking like a thick Pocahontas. At home, I was just Miyona. I liked it that way, because I would never act the way I do in the streets in front of my children.

...

Hearing sirens brought me back to present time, as I hauled ass away from the body. I cut behind a house and jumped over the fence. Don't get it twisted; just because I was thick didn't mean that I wasn't good on my feet. After I was a good distance, I pulled my burner phone out my bra and called the homies up. After telling them where I was, I posted up and waited for them. Five minutes later, they were pulling up, so I quickly jumped in, and they sped off.

We went back to the trap so I could change my clothes and grab my car. After I handled all that, I headed home. I was excited when I pulled up at the same time that Juelz did. He owned an auto body shop, as well as being in the streets, so it was really no telling what time he was coming home. All I knew was that he never let the sun beat him home, and I appreciated that.

I parked the car, grabbed my purse and keys, then hopped out the car. I walked right over to Juelz. He looked like he had got a fresh shape up and his dreads retwisted. Damn, my baby was sexy. I stood on my tippy toes and kissed his lips before grabbing his hand and damn near pulling him inside the house. We walked in and was greeted by both of our sons and their nanny playing around. I looked at my phone and saw that it was past their bedtime, but I wasn't in the mood to argue about it so I let it slide.

"Mommy!" Our baby boy Makhi ran to us. He was four years old and a momma's boy, while Juelz Jr, our little five-year-old, was all about his father. He acted like him and everything. He looked like him, too, with my complexion. Well, both of the kids had my complexion; they just didn't look like me.

"What you doing?" I asked him as I picked him up.

"Mommy, I play horsey." He said, while laughing since I was tickling him.

"Awe. You are? How about you finish playing horsey tomorrow, and you get ready for bed now." I carried him towards the stairs.

"Yes, Mommy. I was waiting for you." He told me, and I shook my head because I should have known better.

I realized that he was already in his pajamas, so I took him to his room. Laying him down in his bed, I kicked my shoes off, because I already knew what was coming next. He was about to ask me to lay with him. I made sure to lay on top of the covers since I had just come from outside. I laid with him until he fell asleep, which was about five minutes later. Then, I kissed him on the forehead before grabbing my shoes and walking out the room.

I knew that Jr was following his dad around, so I didn't even bother to call him and tell him to go to bed. Instead, I headed to my room for a much-needed shower. I turned the water on before stripping my clothes off. I wanted the water to be nice and hot when I stepped in.

After a nice warm shower, I wrapped the towel around me and headed into my room. I sat on the bench that was on the edge of my bed and started to put some lotion on my body. As I applied lotion to my body, the only thing on my mind was what I was going to do the next day with my kids. I kind of wanted to have a family day, but at the same time, I wanted to just have a mom's day with my boys.

I grabbed my nightgown and slipped it on before going to my side of the bed and climbing in. I grabbed the remote and channel surfed while I waited on Juelz to come in the room. About a half hour later, he came walking in with a towel around his waist.

"Why did you shower in the hallway bathroom?" I asked him.

"I don't know. I just did." He shrugged, as he headed into the closet. He came back out with a pair of boxers on his ass. I was sitting up because something about the way he acting wasn't sitting right with me. "Why you looking like that?"

"You okay? You look like something is wrong."

"Some shit with work…" He said, and I stopped him.

"No talking about work at home. But whatever it is that is bothering you, I hope you feel better. Come here and let me give you a massage. Let wifey make you feel better." I smiled at him, then he laid across the bed on his stomach, and I crawled over and sat on his back. I leaned back and grabbed the remote before handing it to him. Of course, he turned to ESPN. I didn't mind, though. I was happy if bae was happy.

I started to rub on his back. As I worked his shoulders, I leaned forward and brought my tongue to his ear. I licked his lobe making him lightly moan out. I knew that was his spot.

"Chill, Mimi, before you end up on your back with them thick ass, caramel thighs on my shoulders."

"Maybe that's how I want to end up." I said, seductively, before kissing her ear.

"Oh my gosh!" I yelled out when he flipped me backwards on my back. I looked up at him giggling hard as hell.

"Look what you did." He pointed at his dick, which was coming through the hole in his boxers.

"I like it, though." I licked my lips.

"Keep on. I'mma stick him in, and you gon' be screaming and everything, then you going to be hoarse in the morning."

"I don't think you doing all that." I lied.

My baby held it all the way down in the bedroom. Like ten toes deep into the mattress down. I watched as he pulled his boxers off before pulling my nightgown over my head. Fuck foreplay. He spread my legs wide open before ramming all eleven, thick inches inside of me before closing them enough for each leg to be over his shoulders. He gave me no mercy as he moved in and out of me. I felt every piece of him in me.

"S-slow down, please." I moaned out.

"Nah, Mimi. Talk that shit now. Say what you were saying."

"I said Papi dick be so good. Shiiiiit, you, fat dick bastard." I moaned.

"Uh-hmm. Ya shit must have been ready. You all wet and shit. Just how I like it."

"Shit! Just like that." I tried to move one of my legs down, but he had a tight grip on the both of them where I couldn't. Oh my gosh. I'm going to cum. I swear I am." I yelled out."

"Did I tell you to? You better not! I swear your ass talk hell of shit but can't ever back it up when I get this dick in you." He taunted. I hated when he started doing all of that shit, because he right. I do talk a lot of shit, and he be ripping me when it all goes down.

"Shh! Yes, Papi. Just like that!" I moaned, as I was cumming. I couldn't help it. He was working too hard.

"Oh, you want to be hardheaded, right?" He flipped me on my stomach. I laid still as he lifted my ass up with my chest still on the mattress. He rammed himself deep inside of me. My kitty was still sensitive from me cumming. He didn't care, though; he gave me them deep, deadly strokes. I was glad when he let go inside of me. That was the best feeling ever when he fell out on my back. I turned my head to meet his lips. Then, I tongue kissed him as he rolled off of me, pulling me closer to him so that we could get under the cover. I got comfortable on his chest and was about to dose off.

Andrea

"Mimi, you sleep?" Juelz asked.

"I was about to be. Why, what's up?" I looked up at him. He was looking at me with a blank look on his face.

"Question. How come you haven't started planning our wedding yet? You don't want to marry me?"

"I just figured that you weren't ready. I mean, we been engaged for a while, and you never really brought the whole thing up. I'm ready whenever." I let him know.

"I'm ready for you to officially be my wife. We already got the family, and you the only one with a different last name. So, we need to get this moving. I don't like that your last name is something different than our sons." He told me with base in his voice.

"I didn't know if you were ready or not. Like I said, we been engaged for a while now. You haven't said too much. I just thought that you weren't ready yet." I told him in defense. I didn't like the way he was grilling me.

"That sound dumb as fuck! Why the fuck wouldn't I want to hurry and marry your ass? We been together for years, and we got two kids. Last, but not least, we lay in the same bed every fucking night after you do your wifely duties. So please explain the dumb shit to me!" He was mad. I hated when Juelz got mad, because it was like his voice was so powerful that it shook the walls. It was sexy but slightly scary at the same time.

"Okay, Juelz! I'm not about to argue with you! You getting tight for what! I'm not about to argue with you. I'm going to bed so I can spend the day with my babies tomorrow. So goodnight!" I moved away from him and rolled over near the edge of the bed. I got comfortable and let myself drift off to sleep.

Chapter 2: Juelz Johnson

I looked at Miyonna as she rolled over and went to sleep. I loved the hell out of her ass, and everyone knew it, but she just pissed me the fuck off. She was acting like she didn't want to be my wife, but she needed to let me know what was up.

I looked at her once more before I got out the bed, then I grabbed my weed and a wrap before heading out the room, downstairs to the basement. I sat on the couch and got comfortable before grabbing the remote and cutting the television on. I turned to the news and cut the volume down while I rolled up. I lit my blunt and laid back.

Everything ran through my head as I smoked. Miyonna being the main subject. I knew that I wanted to be with her ass forever. Maybe I needed to plan the whole damn wedding and have it as a surprise for her. As a man, it wasn't easy to bare your feelings, then be a man and have niggas respect you. Then not look at you like you was soft. For instance, what Miyonna did as work. A lot of niggas would be intimidated, but I was secure with my shit. She never tried to belittle me or act like I wasn't a man. Plus, we kept that shit away from home. Yeah, she was my connect, but at home, she was my lady and the mother of my kids. Street shit stayed in the streets.

A Lady in the Sheets, A Savage in the Streets

On some real shit, I liked that we agreed to keep street shit in the streets, but sometimes, when I was stressed out, I wished like hell I could vent to my better half. She does shit to make me feel better or at least try and help, but it was whatever. After smoking my whole blunt, I headed back to my room, where Miyonna was knocked out, so I got in bed and did the same thing.

Waking up later in the morning, it was quiet as hell throughout the house, and when I reached my hand out, I felt that it was empty. I opened my eyes and sat up. It didn't take a genius to see that Miyonna was gone and took the kids with her. I grabbed my phone and tried to call her, but she wasn't answering. I then remembered that she said that she was spending time with the boys today, so I hung up before the voicemail kicked in. I got out the bed, went to handle my hygiene, then got dressed to start my day.

After getting my shit together, I headed out the door. Once I hopped in my car, I called my nigga Montè up. I decided to just go kick it with him since I really ain't have shit else to do.

"Yo?" He answered like he was busy.

"What's good, Slime? I'm 'bout to come scoop you and shit. Be ready in like five."

"Word. I'mma be outside."

"Alright. One."

Andrea

"One." I hung up, then turned my radio on and let my music bang. I ain't give a fuck that it was 10:00 a.m. Shit, it was time to get up and get it. The early bird catches the worm.

Exactly five minutes later, I pulled up to my nigga house, and he was standing outside like he was impatiently waiting for me to get there. I barely stopped the car before he was hopping in. He did his usual of leaning the seat back and getting comfortable.

"What's good?" I asked him.

"Ain't shit. Same shit, different day. You know how it go." Montè answered before sitting up and dapping me up. He then laid right back.

"Why was you standing outside like some groupie?" I asked with a chuckle.

"Ameerah on that bullshit early in the morning. Don't nobody have time for that shit. Princess up just looking and shit. Then, Ameerah started throwing shit which scared Princess and she started crying. You know Ameerah crazy!" He laughed.

Montè and Ameerah were Miyonna and my best friends. He was my right-hand man on the business side, and we had been friends for years. Ameerah and Miyonna had been friends since they were younger, so just imagine how ironic it was when Miyonna and I started fucking with each other. It was a small world for real. Ameerah didn't know that Miyonna was a connect. That was something that she kept away from her, because she considered Ameerah as a part of her 'home' life.

"Damn! I hope you was ducking, Nigga!" I joked.

"I sure was. I started heading for the door. You know she won't come outside acting a fucking fool. She doesn't want people in our business so she chills on that." He said. I just nodded. I minded my business when it came to other people's business and relationships, but them niggas was always at it. It didn't matter, because by the end of the night, they were back to the peacefulness and fucking each other. That's why no one paid them no mind.

"We bout to go get something to eat, cuz my stomach touching my back, and I wanna talk to you about something." I told Montè, as I pulled up into Amy's parking lot.

We sat down at the table, and I was ready to order, but of course Montès' mind was somewhere else. He was ready to talk about whatever was on my mind.

"So what's good? Is it business?"

"Nah. This personal business. Shit with Miyonna and I." I let him know, and his vibe changed. Not in a bad way.

"Oh, what's going on?" Montè be focused as hell when people talking to him. That was a good thing, but it was kind of funny at the same time.

"Let's order first." I told him just as the waiter walked up to our table. We both ordered and waited for her to go to the back before I started talking.

Andrea

"You know I'm a street nigga, from head to toe. I ain't expect for Miyonna and me to make it this far. Well, as far as we made it when I proposed a few years back. Anyway, the other night, a thought popped into my head. Like, why she not planning the wedding..." I said, and Montè cut me off.

"You think it's some fishy shit going on?" He asked.

"Hold on. Let me finish." He nodded. "Anyway, I ask her. She gon' give me some bullshit talking 'bout she wasn't sure if I was ready! I'm like yo, Miyonna, are you fucking serious right now! We been in this muthafucking relationship for years. If I wasn't ready for marriage, why the fuck would I fucking propose? She had me pissed the fuck off! There ain't shit dumb about that girl, so I don't know why she was trying to act dumb." I explained. I was started to get pissed again thinking about it.

"Wow. I don't even know what to say. Like, is she serious?" He asked.

"Yeah. She was." I told him, as the waiter came back with our food. I deaded the conversation and ate my food. I didn't want stranger mothafuckas in my business. We sat and quietly talked about business. We talked about shipments and new team members. We had to welcome them in, in style.

After we were done, I paid the bill, and we headed to the trap to check out the lil' homies and see what they were up to. I liked to pop up on my workers and stay in the mix. As a boss, you should always check on your business. I had to make sure things were flowing right.

14

"This a raid! Show me your hands!" I yelled, as I walked in and saw that niggas weren't on their job. They all looked at me like I was crazy.

"Damn, big Homie! We ain't even realize y'all was here." One of the lil' homies said.

"I know! That's why I said what I said. Tighten that shit up!" I let them know.

"That's our bad! We had counted and shit. Then, niggas started betting on the game and what not."

"Alright. Stay on your P's and Q's at all times. It doesn't matter what you doing. Stay alert! Niggas could have busted in and started busting. Y'all niggas could have been Swiss cheese in this bitch." I said with a serious face.

"We got you, Big Homie." I just nodded, then went and grabbed a chair to sit in. I looked around the room before speaking up.

"I'm scheduling a meeting for later on in the week. Niggas getting too comfortable so we about to switch some shit up. The lil' niggas out here that be sticking shit up gon' memorize y'all routines and shit gon get real so the meeting gon' be about new positions and locations and shit. Let y'all little crews know. The whole team needs to be at this meeting. The day of this meeting, the streets better be dryer than a fiend's lips. Ya heard?"

"We got you!" They all said in unison. I nodded once again.

Andrea

"Alright! I'm 'bout to be out. I'll hit yall in a few days. Tighten this shit up!" I said, as I made my way to the door. Montè was right behind me. We hopped in my car, and I let my radio bang, as I made my way to drop him off. I looked at the clock and saw that it was a little after one in the afternoon. I was just going to go home and chill while Miyonna was out the boys.

We pulled up to Montè and Ameerah's house, and I had to blink twice. The scene in front of me was too much. These niggas, man!

"Yo, stay here, my nigga! I might need you in case shit get ugly." Montè said, as he was about to jump out the car. I glared at him, because he knew damn well I didn't like getting in people's business. "For real! It's gon' get real! I don't know who she thinks she is throwing my shit outside like this."

I just shook my head and sat there like a real nigga would. I watched as he walked to the front door and tried to use his key to open it, but the door didn't budge. Next thing I know, he started banging on and kicking the door while yelling.

"Open the fucking door! Why the fuck would you change the locks, man!" He yelled up at the window. I followed his glare and saw that Ameerah was in the window looking down at him.

"Fuck you, Montè! You wanna cheat with these bitches! Go right the fuck ahead. All your shit is on the front lawn. You better hurry up before people start taking it, before they see the free sign on it!" She yelled back. I couldn't believe she

16

had all his shit on the lawn with a 'For Sale' sign in front of it; the word 'free' was written on it. I just shook my head.

"I'm advising your ass to come and open the door. If I have to break in, I'm fucking you up! I promise that shit." These niggas are like Ike and Tina. The crazy part was that they were going to be fucking by later on tonight.

"Fuck you, Montè! Go fuck with one of them other bitches you be fucking with. I'm done!" She yelled, and he fell out laughing. I had to chuckle myself. She said that shit all the time.

"You say that now, then later when my dick deep in you, it's a whole other story. You only done for a few hours." He said through laughter.

"Whatever!" She gave him the finger.

"Alright, Ameerah! I'm not about to play with you. I'mma get my shit then go find me a new bitch to fuck with. My daughter 'bout to have a whole stepmom, so when you get mad, just know that you told me to go with a new bitch. It's all your fault." Montè said, and I fell out laughing, as he walked to where his stuff was and picked up a few bags before heading towards my truck. I tried to stop laughing, but it was impossible. He opened the back door and proceeded to put the bags in when the house door opened up, and Ameerah came running out.

"Bae No! I'm sorry! I'll chill out! I promise." Ameerah pleaded, and I tried to hold my laughter in. That didn't work, though. I even tried to bite my lip to keep from laughing, but

17

that wasn't working either. I had tears in my eyes from laughing so hard.

"Fuck that, Ameerah! I'm sick of this shit. It's a pattern. Every few days, your ass get to acting crazy and shit. Accusing me of shit. I'mma get tired of it and really do shit since you keep saying it. Move man!" He put all the bags in and walked to get some more. She started taking the bags out and headed towards the house, while I was still laughing.

"Bae, just come in the house." Ameerah pleaded once again.

"Nah. I'm going to my bachelor pad. I'll come see Princess tomorrow." Montè smirked. That made me laugh more, because she played right into his shit.

"No the fuck you not! I will beat your ass, and the bitch you trying to be with."

"Chill. If I come in, you gon' chill, right?"

"Yeah." Montè looked at me and smirked before taking his shit inside. After he took all the shit out my car, I pulled out the driveway and headed home.

...

Kicking my shoes off, I grabbed my wrap and weed. I rolled while watching ESPN highlights. This was the earliest I ever been in the house. I guess that was, cuz I ain't have much to do for the day. As I smoked, I couldn't help but laugh as I thought about Ameerah and Montè's ass. Them niggas will have your stomach hurting.

I ended up smoking myself to sleep, but I woke up to the smell of food being cooked. I looked at the time and saw that it was after six o'clock. That meant that Miyonna and the boys were home. I got up and headed into the bathroom to wash my face and brush my teeth before heading upstairs. I walked into the kitchen and saw my younger son sitting at the kitchen table coloring. I walked over and dapped him up before following the sounds of my older son. He was in the living room with a bunch of trucks and cars playing. I dapped him up before letting him go back to playing. I walked back to the kitchen and walked towards Miyonna.

"So, you didn't see me standing here?" She asked while glaring at me.

"You saw me walking towards you. Chill."

"No! You didn't say shit to me. You just went to our kids without saying a word to me. You still mad at me?"

"No. Relax with that shit, for real!" I told her with bass, and she rolled her eyes before turning her head away from me. "Roll em again!" I grabbed her by the waist and pulled her closer to me before wrapping my arms around her. I kissed her along the neck to where her spot was making her lightly moan out. I smirked, cuz I was *that* nigga. I knew she was wet, so I reached my hand inside her pants to make sure. *I knew it!*

"Stop. That's so unsanitary. Plus, the kids."

"Now, it's unsanitary. You weren't saying that before when I would lay you across the table and eat that shit like you was a meal. Or when the kids were napping that day and you had

19

that one leg on the counter, and I was ripping that from behind while playing with your clit. Juices flying all in this mothafucka. It wasn't unsanitary then. Now was it?"

"Shh. Y-yes it was." She was barely audible as I played with her clit. "The b-boys." She shuttered. I dipped two fingers inside of her while using my thumb to rub on her clit.

"You like this shit, don't you?" I whispered in her ear before biting her lobe.

"I'm c-cumming!" She moaned out loud.

"Shhhh, girl. The boys, remember!" I taunted in her ear.

"Where we going, Mommy?" I heard my oldest son ask, and I fell out laughing as I pulled my hand out of her jeans. I held her as her legs buckled.

"Yeah. Where we going, Mommy?" I mocked with a smirk. She looked at me and rolled her eyes. "Go clean yourself up. I bet you stop playing with me now." I told her. I washed my hands at the sink before walking over to my youngest prince to sit down.

"You wanna color, Daddy?" He asked while handing me a crayon.

"Yeah, man. What we coloring?" I asked him.

"This!" He pointed at the book making me laugh. His little ass got excited with everything, and I loved to see him happy. We colored, and he started to tell me about his day, and I laughed as he tried pronouncing words that he knew he couldn't. I turned around when I heard footsteps behind me and saw that Miyonna had changed her clothes. She rolled her eyes hard at me.

"I ain't gon say nun to you. Just remember that you sleep with me every night." I smirked at her, and her facial expression changed. Miyonna knew what it was. My dick game was official, and she knew it.

"Dinner's almost done." She announced in a low voice before walking over and sitting on my lap.

"What?"

"So why Ameerah's phone dialed me, and all I hear is them fucking in the background when I answered." She said for only me to hear.

"I figured that. She threw all that nigga's clothes out on the front lawn with a free sign in front of it. He said he was gon' leave her then. Shit went left!"

"I bet your black ass was laughing like you always do."

"I sure was! They funny as hell! You know they are, too." I laughed just thinking about them. They will turn anybody's day from shit to hilarious.

"Yeah they are. I'm waiting for her to call me for real to tell me about it. Like she always does." Baby sighed, and I laughed.

"How was your day today?"

"Tiring. The boys and I went damn near everywhere. I need a body rub." She kissed my forehead before leaning in near my ear. "And some head."

"You got it. You really didn't need to tell me, cuz I was gon' do that anyway. The way your ass was sitting in them jeans had me like, damn! You definitely getting the stiffness tonight."

"I think I want another baby." She blurted out, and I looked at her. She had me fucked up. We not having no more babies until she gets my last name.

"Nope! You already know why, too."

"I have baby fever."

"I got wedding fever. So, what you saying?" I asked her.

"I'm ready whenever."

"Alright." Was all I said.

"Let's eat so we can bathe the boys and stuff." She smiled.

I was ready to spend some more time with my sons before I spent the rest of the night with my lady. She doesn't even know that tonight she really 'bout to be sore, cuz she keeps fucking with me.

Chapter 3: Monte Washington

"Fuck! Baybee, just like that!" Ameerah screamed, as I was fucking her from the back.

"Throw that shit back, Meerah! Stop fucking with me!" I smacked her healthy ass.

"I'm 'bout to cum, bae. Shiiiit!" She cussed as she fell out, but I wasn't done yet. I grabbed her right leg and held it up as I pumped in and out of her. Her pussy was tight and warm. Just how I liked it. I gripped her waist tight letting everything go inside of her knocking the wind out of me. I laid on her back kissing her neck.

"Pussy good as fuck!" I told her as I rolled off of her.

"I love you, baby." She rolled over and laid on my chest.

"I know. I love you, too." I kissed her forehead. This was Ameerah and me. She turns up on a nigga every few days, and we always end up fucking at the end of the argument. Ameerah and I been together for five years. I can't say it's been the best, cuz I was a foul ass nigga to her in the beginning. I cheated on her, and she caught me. She left a nigga for a couple of months, and I was sick. I ain't tell her that, though. I felt like that old saying, 'you don't know what you got till it's gone'. That was an understatement.

She took me back, and I been in the straight ever since. I couldn't blame her for being insecure, because I caused it, but it's really annoying, especially after all these years. Then, I think my baby just naturally crazy. I couldn't be mad, though. She's a Black and Indian fireball. She will turn up on somebody quick, but I loved that about her. My baby stands at five foot four. She was a thick 'ems. She wasn't as thick as Miyonna, but she wasn't lacking either. She had curves and weight in the right places.

"Are you mad at me?" Ameerah asked, snapping me out my thoughts.

"No. I'm good now. Why you ask?"

"I was talking to you, and you were ignoring me."

"My bad. I was deep in thought about something." I let her know.

"Thinking about what?"

"Let it go. It's business."

"Uh, whatever! I'm about to go check on Princess then cook." She said, as she slowly got up off of me. I watched as her ass jiggled when she walked. My baby was the shit, and she knew it. When she walked in the bathroom, I grabbed the remote and channel surfed. Wasn't shit on, so I just got up and turned my game on. I heard small footsteps, so I hurried up and threw some boxers on, because I knew it was my daughter. She ran into the room and tried to jump on the bed. At four years old, Princess was very active. She will jump on anything that she could. She just liked to move around. That was her thing.

"What you doing, Princess?"

"I want chips, Daddy. The brown ones that taste good."

"The barbecue?"

"Yes!" She smiled, and I had to smile too. I stared, smiling at her for a minute before my smile faded. She noticed that it was fading away, too. "What'sta matter Daddy? You sad?"

"No. Daddy is fine." I leaned in and tickled her making her laugh uncontrollably.

"O-okay. S-stop, Daddy." She stuttered getting it out because she was still laughing hard as hell.

"Okay. I quit." I told her.

"Me, too." Princess said, as Ameerah was walking out the bathroom. I'm glad that she had put her robe on.

"What you in here doing to my baby?" She walked over and jumped on me.

"We just playing." I looked at her. "I hope you about to put some clothes on." I couldn't lie and say that I wasn't territorial about Ameerah because I was. I didn't like other niggas in her face. I ain't like not knowing where she was either. I really didn't like the fact that she worked, but my baby was ambitious, so what could I do about it? I just sucked it up and talked to her in between house showings. She is a real estate agent.

"You act like you got company coming over or something. It's just you, me, and Princess."

"You never know. I don't want nobody stealing glances at you."

Andrea

"They already do." She mumbled, as she walked in the closet. I got up and followed behind her, because I thought I was hearing things.

"What you say?"

"Nothing, man! Let it go. It was just business." Ameerah smirked, as she pulled a pair of shorts on and a black tank top.

"Keep on and watch what happens." I warned her.

"You gon' spank me, Daddy?" She moved closer to me grabbing my dick. "I like when you spank me while slamming into me from the back. When my ass jiggles, it sends a vibration to my clit, which turns me on more." She squeezed my dick how I liked it before letting go. He got hard.

"Nah. Gon' head and close that closet door. You not even about to do me like that then walk off." I looked at her like I was telling her to do it right now. She knew what was up, because she walked over, closed the door, and locked it before walking back to me. I pulled her shorts down and rubbed her clit making her wetter before picking her up and putting her on the table that we had in the closet. Placing her on her hands and knees, I pushed her upper body down where her ass was up in the air. I blew on her clit before putting my whole face in it. Giving special attention to her clit, I sucked it into my mouth making her wet as hell and driving her crazy. When I felt her body tense up, I pulled my dick out and rammed it deep inside of her.

"Shhhh. Bae! Oh my gosh!" She moaned out.

"Be quiet. You know Princess in the other room." I told her, as I reached around and rubbed on her clit.

"Bastard! Oh my fucking god! Right th-there, baby!"

"What's right there?" I kept stroking.

"My-my sp-spot, Daddy! You big dick fucker!" She screamed out, as I kept digging her back out. "I'm cumming! Oh my god!" She called out.

"Let it rain on daddy." I told her before gripping her waist. I got a good grip and drilled the fuck out of Ameerah. Not before long, I was busting too. I stayed inside of her until I was drained. She was gon' be pregnant soon. I already knew it. After catching my breath, I pulled out of Ameerah and helped her down off the table. I laughed as she tried to stand on wobbled legs.

"Help me! Can you carry me into the bathroom?" She asked, and I just looked at her. I really didn't know why she asked. I could see that she could barely walk. Thank god there was a door from the closet that we could use to walk in the bathroom. Princess did not need to see this.

"I got you." I scooped her up and carried her into the bathroom. Turning the shower on, I let it heat up so we could get in. I looked at Ameerah, and she looked like she had something deep on her mind. I pulled her close, and she rested her head on my shoulder.

"What's wrong with you?" I asked her and she shrugged her shoulders. "Nah, talk!" She released a long sigh.

"Fine. Are you cheating on me?" She asked, and I felt warm liquid on my chest. It didn't take a genius to figure out that she was crying. I used my pointer finger and thumb to grab her hold of her chin and lift her head up to look at me.

"Ameerah, I swear on Princess that I am not cheating. Been there and done that! I'm not off that no more. You the only one I want and need. Besides, your pussy way better than what them hoes were. Alright?" I looked her deep in her eyes so that she knew that I was serious as hell.

"Okay." I kissed her forehead.

"Why you thinking that?" I was curious.

"You been acting strange lately. Like walking out the room when you on the phone. Then whispering. Then you staying out extra late and shit. That's the same shit you were doing when you was creeping." She said, and I shook my head.

"Trust me, it's business. You know I don't like to talk business around you. I respect you too much to get caught up in my shit. As far as staying out late, I be working, making sure shit straight. I will make it a point to come home at a better time, okay?"

"Yeah. Love you, Mont."

"I love you, too. Now, come on." I pulled her in the shower. I had to get one more quickie while in the shower. My baby pussy was grade A+.

...

We had eaten dinner, and Princess was off to bed so we were chilling, curled up watching a movie on the couch. Just

28

as the movie was getting good, the doorbell rang. I ain't know who it was, but I was about to see. I grabbed the remote and hit the channel for me to see the cameras. I jumped up when I saw that it was one of my little niggas at the door. Shit must have got real. I hurried to the door to see what was going on. I opened the door, and Man rushed in.

"My bad, Big Homie, to barge in like this, but you weren't answering the phone..." I cut him off.

"What's going on?"

"We took a hit. Money missing. You or Ju wasn't answering, so I came through."

"Y'all know who took it?" I asked.

"Yes and No!" He answered.

"The fuck that mean?"

"We know who took it, but it had to be someone who sent him to do it. Nigga was acting too weird. We got him hemmed up at the spot, but he not saying too much. That nigga took the money somewhere. We don't know where. He was on the phone talking 'bout it to them when we overheard him."

"What the fuck! None of this is making sense to me. Let me put some clothes on then we can head out. Stay here."

I left Man standing near the door, as I turned around and headed up the stairs to my room. I hurried and threw on an all-black sweatsuit and my black Timbs before grabbing my heat and heading back downstairs. Nothing was making sense to me at all. I walked back in the living room, and it didn't take a genius to see that Ameerah overheard the conversation that I had with Man. She looked mad as hell, but I had to go and handle business. I went and sat next to her on the couch.

"Yo, Ma, I gotta go handle some shit right quick. I'll be back as soon as possible. Go get in the bed. I don't want you down here by yourself. Alright?"

"Whatever, Montè! I don't know why I deal with this shit. It's always something." She snapped as she stood up. I couldn't even be mad at her. I pulled her close to me and kissed her on the forehead before she headed up the stairs. I grabbed the remote and turned the television off before heading out the living room.

"Come on, Man! Let's be out! You can explain this shit to me in the car." I told him as we headed out. I hopped in the passenger's seat of his car, and he started to run the story down, as I called Juelz up and told him to meet me at the spot. It was about to be one long ass night. I hoped Ameerah slept her attitude off by the time I got back to the house.

Chapter 4: Ameerah Statum

I stomped my ass all the way up the stairs when Montè left. He pissed me the fuck off. Every time we were chilling together, his ass always had some business to handle, and I hated that about him. He didn't know how and when to separate the two. I worked and owned a whole business but still put aside decent time for my family. This nigga ain't know how to do that. I loved my nigga with everything that I had inside of me. Some people say that I am weak, but I disagree. I'm just deep in love with a hood nigga.

Montè and I been through the storm, from his ass cheating, to my ass leaving, but we were able to weather the storm. Something inside of me is telling me that his ass is cheating again, because he doing the shit that he was doing before. Then, he wonders why I be ready to throw his shit outside on the curb. I wouldn't argue with his ass outside, but I would surely put his stuff outside. I really didn't know how much longer I could put up with this shit.

As soon as I walked inside of my room, I grabbed my cell phone to call my best friend Miyonna. I knew that I could talk to her, and she wouldn't be biased about anything. I was so glad when she answered on the second ring.

"Yes, Drama Queen? I mean, Meerah." She laughed, and I had to laugh, too. I stopped and sighed deeply, and she knew what was up.

"He makes me sick!" I said to her, and she chuckled.

"What happened? Cuz last I heard, y'all was fucking. I mean, your ass dialed me and everything."

"Yeah, we made love. Everything was good all day, then about five minutes ago, one of their homies came and said they got robbed, and once again, his ass was out the door..." I started to say, but then she cut me off.

"Ameerah, why you getting mad? You knew what he was into since the first day y'all met. What's really good?"

"I think he cheating on me again." I told her.

"Oh, Lord! Wait a minute! You said that they got robbed?" She asked in a panic.

"Yeah. That's what Man came over and said..." I started to run the conversation down to her, but she cut me off.

"I'mma call you right back." Miyonna said then hung up.

She was acting weird as hell. I guess I was going to wait for her to call me back. I went and got my tablet off the dresser before crawling into bed. I got comfortable and pulled up my kindle app so I could find something to read. I scrolled and saw that my favorite author Andrea had a new book called *Crazy Bout This Block Boy: A Teenage Love* out, so I clicked on it and got ready for the emotional wave that she would take me on with her characters.

A Lady in the Sheets, A Savage in the Streets

I was reading good as hell and about Drianna. I could fuck with her young ass, because she was a fireball with a smart ass mouth. I was getting to the part when she was walking up on her friend Tisha at the lockers when my phone rang. I was mad as hell for a second. When I realized that it was Miyonna calling, I sat my kindle to the side and answered the phone.

"What's up, girl? What you doing?" Her voice had changed. She didn't sound the way that she did when she had hung up the phone on me.

"Nothing. I was waiting for you to call me and reading Andrea's new book. That shit fire so far."

"Oh, damn! I gotta cop it. Alright, so what was you telling me about Montè?" She asked. I could tell that she was in bed comfortable as hell. Her voice said it all.

"I think his ass cheating. He acting how he was acting before when he was."

"Hell, nah! You wanna do a stake-out? Bitch, you know I got you."

"Not really, Mimi. I don't want to go looking for something and get more than what I bargained for. You know that what's done in the dark comes to the light."

"Ain't that the truth. But for real, don't be stressing over anything. You want to wait to let shit drop on your lap, so you can't be a bitch to Montè. What if what you feeling is wrong? You just need to chill. I want us to have a girls' day out, so that we can talk for real. I don't like how you be crying and carrying on after you provoke him. That's not cool." She started on that big sister role, and I hated that about her. She would start giving out advice like she was really somebody's parent. Granted, she was older than me, but we were both grown.

"Alright. I could use some retail therapy." I let her know.

"Cool. I'm tired as hell trying to stay awake. I will call you in the morning. Be easy, and don't start with Montè when he come in. Take your ass to sleep. Love you!"

"Love you, too." I told her before hanging up the phone. I put it on the charger and picked up my tablet. I read until my eyes had a mind of their own, and I dozed off to sleep.

...

Waking up the next morning, I thought that I had overslept until I heard Montè's loud ass snoring. I peeked over at the clock and saw that it was going on eight. I laid there for a little while longer before getting up to go and handle my hygiene and going to cook breakfast. I knew that Princess was about to be up within the next half hour. She was a diva about her food.

Walking in the kitchen, I headed over to the fridge to pull out breakfast stuff. Just as I was cracking the eggs, I heard the house phone ring. I walked over to it and looked at the caller ID and saw that it was saying unknown. I grabbed it to answer it, and the caller hung up before I could. A few minutes later, it rang again in my hands. This time, I answered and said hello. No one said anything back, but I could hear heavy breathing before a low laugh, then the phone hung up.

A Lady in the Sheets, A Savage in the Streets

I rolled my eyes at the phone wishing I could roll them at whoever was playing on the phone. It was too early to be doing that. I sat the phone down and went back to what I was doing. A half hour later, I was done with breakfast, and Princess was heading down the stairs.

"Mommy, I think I'm ready to eat." She announced, as she climbed in the chair. I looked at her and could tell that she brushed her teeth and washed her face. She had toothpaste on her shirt

"Okay. Let me go wake daddy up, then we can eat. Okay?" I asked her, and she nodded. I turned and headed out the kitchen. I walked upstairs to my bedroom, and when I walked in, I saw that Montè wasn't in bed. I knew that he was in the bathroom by the water that I heard running. I opened the bathroom door and couldn't help but stare. All I saw was my baby and his chest out.

"What you looking at?"

"What? Huh? Oh, uh breakfast done." I told him while blushing. Just sad that he had this type of effect on me. I turned to walk out when I felt something on my feet. I knew it was the damn dog. That meant that Princess let her ass out. I hated for the dog to run around my floor which is why I kept her in the cage at all times. She only came out when Montè was taking her for a walk.

"Mommy, Kerro can eat, too." Princess said, as she came running in the room.

Andrea

"Go put Kerro back! NOW! Then, wash your hands again." I yelled at her. I shook my head, because it was about to be one long ass day.

"Don't yell at her like that! You obviously frustrated about something else; don't take it out on her. Talk to daddy; what's up?" Montè walked out the bathroom and over to the chair that we had in our room pulling me with him.

"Nothing..." I started to say, but he cut me off.

"Don't say nothing. You still mad from last night?"

"No. I'm over it."

Okay. So what is bothering you? Be real!"

"Somebody was playing on the phone earlier. It annoyed me a little. That's it."

"I'll check it out. That's all you had to say. Now, go make my plate while I walk Kerro." I stood up, and he popped me on the ass. "Ass fat as fuck!"

"I wish you stop."

"Never! You shouldn't be fine as fuck!" I giggled, as we walked out the room. I headed back to the kitchen to get my family squared away so I could get dressed then go get up with Miyonna and have some much-needed girl time.

...

"Mimi!" I yelled out, excitedly, when I spotted Miyonna in the store. Of course, we were doing some retail therapy.

"Meerah!" She was just as excited. "Look at you bitch. Looking thicker than a Snicker."

36

"I know you ain't talking. You thicker than me!" I said back with a bunch of laughter.

"You crazy!" We both laughed. "What's going on?"

"Nothing. People playing on phones early in the morning and shit. Like, the fuck! Why people ain't got nothing better to do with their time?" Shit, I was annoyed just thinking about it.

"Damn! You think it has something to do with the guys and being robbed?"

"Damn! I didn't even think of that until now. Wow! Montè said that he was going to handle it, so I'mma let him do that."

"That's good. So I have been having baby fever, but Ju doesn't want another one until we are married..." I had to cut her off.

"I don't blame him. You have no reason as to why y'all ain't married. Shit, at least he thinks about marriage. Montè hasn't mentioned one word about it."

"To be honest friend, I think I am scared. Like, my dad isn't here to walk me down the aisle. It wouldn't be right."

"I'm 'bout to smack the hell out of you. I swear!"

"You don't understand!"

"So make me!"

"I feel like it is traditional for a father to walk their daughter down the aisle. Our marriage could possibly fail..." I had to cut her off.

"Are you kidding me? This a joke? You telling me that y'all marriage going to fail because your dad isn't here to walk you down the aisle?" I couldn't help but fall out laughing. I didn't even care that people were staring or looking hard at me.

"You don't have to do all that!" She looked embarrassed.

"I do. To prove to you how stupid you sound." I told her. Shit, she did sound stupid.

"Whatever!" She rolled her eyes at me.

"Now you mad? Anyways, all I'm going to say is this, and I'mma be done with it… you can't sit here and say that y'all not going to have a good marriage because your dad not here. If that was the case, look at all the people in the world. Look at all the people who never met their parents, period, and still managed to go on and have a happy and successful life filled with love. You can't let that determine anything. Okay?"

"I guess you are right. I guess I am a little scared." She confessed.

"You think?" I laughed. We walked through the mall shopping and enjoying our time together before Miyonna announced that she had to go and take care of something. I wasn't ready to go home yet, so I headed over to my office.

When I walked in my office, I sat down and looked at all the paper on my desk. I had a schedule for times that I had houses to show. I shook my head and let out a long ass sigh, because I only worked a few days a week, so that meant that I was going to be working from early morning til damn near night time. I guess Montè was going to have something to say about that. In all reality, he didn't want me to work at all, but I wasn't the type to be somewhere sitting on my ass. I was a very independent, go-getter. So eventually we came to a compromise. I could only work a few days a week, but I was fine with that, though. Spending time with my daughter and my man meant everything to me.

After going through papers and grabbing what I needed, I headed home. I had to go and handle my motherly and wifely duties. As soon as I walked into the house, I wanted to turn around and walk right out. Princess had toys everywhere. The house was all turned around. I just looked and shook my head. I couldn't even deal with it, so I just headed upstairs to my bedroom. I wasn't even hungry.

Walking in my room, I stripped down to my bra and panties then climbed onto my bed. Pulling out my laptop, I started to log in my schedule for all my up and coming house showings, including the amenities that they want with their homes. In the middle of my typing, the house phone rang. I reached over and grabbed it. Without looking, I answered it. There was heavy breathing on the phone like it was before. Then, the person mumbled something before giggling and hanging up. I could tell that it was a female. That just pissed me off. Monte` happened to walk in as I slammed the phone down.

"What is wrong with you?" He asked, as he plopped down.

"Somebody playing on the fucking phone again. That shit is annoying, and I didn't know that people still did that dumb ass shit. And I thought that your black ass was going to handle it." I snapped at him. I was annoyed as hell.

"First off, calm the fuck down. Second of all, watch how you talk to me. Third of all, I told you that I was, and I am. Now, how was your day?" He asked, as if he was dismissing me.

"My day started off bad, because someone was playing on the phone, but you knew that already. Then, I was with Miyonna, and my day actually started to turn around. Now I come home, and what do you know. Someone is playing on the phone again!" I wanted to punch his ass, but he would more than likely fuck me up.

"Okay, Ameerah! What are they saying?"

"Nothing. Just breathing hard and laughing. Then hanging up the phone. It must be a bitch of yours."

"Man, shut that shit up! I'm about to go and check on Princess. You finish working so I can have you face down and ass up later on tonight." He said before walking out the room. I stared hard at his back because his ass was guilty of something. I wasn't going to go looking because it was going to drop on my lap soon enough.

Chapter 5: Miyonna Pierce

I was so glad when we were walking in the mall and the subject changed. I could admit that I was a softy on the inside. When it came to street shit, I was as thorough as any dude, but in reality and behind closed doors, I was just as emotional as any other female. I loved Ameerah with all my heart, but who was she to have any say about feelings when she was out here acting hard then crying and begging niggas not to leave her. She was bitch, and like I said, I love her.

After spending most of the day with Ameerah, I had to leave and go transform into to Pocha, because I had a business meeting. Being that I was the connect, when niggas were getting robbed in the streets, it affected me, too. I headed home and changed my clothes. I threw my hair in a bun and headed back out the door. I hopped in my car and headed to the meet-up spot where I met with everyone when it was time to re-up. I walked in the room, and everyone was sitting around. I dapped everyone up before sitting down and getting down to business.

"So I wanted to call this meeting, because it's been a lot going on with people's paper. At the end of the day, we all a team if y'all look at it like that. Everyone's money affects everyone. Look at it like that. If one person's money is short, it affects everyone. If one person's money is short, then it makes me raise everyone's prices so that I have enough to supply everyone else as well as making money for myself. Sounds crazy, but think about it. Nothing can be ignored. I don't care if it's five or five hundred dollars; it's the principal of the situation so the person that got sticky fingers need to be handled. So with the two situations that I know about, are they being taken care of properly?" Looking around the room, I made sure to make eye contact with everyone as I spoke.

"Shit almost taken care of on our end." Macky, one of the guys that I supplied to stated. I looked over at him.

"You and your squad can handle it? You need extra enforcement?"

"No. We got it." He smiled politely. I just simply nodded before continuing to speak.

"Okay. Cool. Well, since everyone is here, I have good news." I smiled. "For a limited time, prices will be dropped. When I say limited, I mean the next time you re-up." I said, and everyone fell out laughing. I was serious, though.

"That's what's up, Pocha! Anything else or we done?"

"We done. Y'all can go!" I dismissed everyone. Once everyone was gone, I looked at my right-hand nigga Dun. He had always been loyal. He was actually a young nigga that ran with my father back in the day. I saw how his loyalty was, and I couldn't help but keep him on the team, but as my right-hand nigga.

"What's up, Pocha?" Dun asked.

"Nothing really. I need you to set up times for everyone's re-up. I will actually do everything else."

"I got you. You know that."

"I know. I'm 'bout to be out. What you about to get into?" I asked him as I stood up and got ready to go.

"Go to be the single man that I am!" I fell out laughing, because this nigga really was a satisfied single. He slept with any female, and as long as you were born with a pussy, you were fuckable in his book. Some of the bitches he smashed were not eye-friendly. I had to admit that they had nice bodies, but looks... hell nah!

"No comment! Have fun! I'm out. Be careful." I walked out the room.

I decided to head and see my mother. We weren't close at all. She hated that I took over my dad's empire. She felt that, since I was female, I shouldn't have. I disagreed with her, and it put a strain on our relationship and been that way ever since my dad died. I call and check on her once in a while and I literally see her maybe twice a year. I didn't have time for her judgmental ass.

After taking the drive, I pulled up to my mother's brick, two-story home. After my dad had died, she decided to take my siblings and live in one of their smaller houses.

I got out the car and stalked up to the front door. Ringing the doorbell, I waited for someone to come and open it. I knew she was home, because there were two cars in the driveway. I was about to walk away when the door swung open. I looked up, and it was my little sister Tiyonna standing there. She had her arms folded like she was annoyed.

"Aw, shoot! Look at the stranger at the doorstep!" She had a smart mouth, and I couldn't stand that shit. She made me want to pop her right in the mouth hard as hell.

"Shut up and move! Where is mommy?" I pushed my way past her and went through the door.

"I'm not telling you! I shouldn't even be talking to strangers. I don't want to be kidnapped." I walked closer to her. I wanted to smack her in the mouth. At sixteen, my little sister was a lot. She was known to fight any and everybody. She did not care. Grown hood niggas would talk about putting her on their team, so I secretly got somebody keeping an eye on her ass.

"Stop trying to kidnap me! Mommy, help me!" She yelled, and my mom came rushing out.

"Tiyonna, shut up!"

"Don't talk to her like that! What are you even doing here in my house? This isn't the normal time for you to stop by." She had attitude in her voice. I wasn't about to deal with her shit.

"I came to check on you. I know that you hate me, but you're still my mother. I do care about your well-being." I matched her tone.

"You couldn't possibly be worried about my well-being." She started to say before turning to Tiyonna. "Let me talk to your sister in private."

44

"Okay." She gladly walked off.

"Like I was saying, if you cared about my well-being, you would have a different career choice. I stress like crazy wondering if something is going to happen to you."

"Why you coming at me like this? If it wasn't me, it would have been Owen or Tiyonna. I just happened to be first born. Nothing has happened to me since I been doing this. I am okay. I keep the two worlds apart. I do what I have to do then I am right back to being simply Miyonna."

"I don't think any female should be out in the world imitating a gangsta. Then when something happens to you, how am I supposed to feel as your mother. You are my oldest daughter, and I constantly worry about you playing gangsta." She snapped.

"Whatever! I'm not a gangsta! More like a savage." I walked towards the front door. "I'm not going to do this with you. I will continue to call you every few months to make sure you are alive." I opened the door and politely walked out. Just as I was about to get in my car, I heard my mother behind me so I turned around.

"Watch your back, Miyonna!" She said, before slamming the door. Something about the way she said it, pissed me off. Jumping in my car, I peeled off. When I stopped at the light, I texted Juelz and asked him to pick the boys up. I wanted to be alone for the moment. I drove all the way home in silence. I knew my dad was turning over in his grave right now with the way me and my mother were with each other.

Andrea

When I got home, I headed inside and straight to my bedroom. Stripping down to my bra and panties, I got in bed and got comfortable under the blankets and sheets. I laid my head on the pillows as thoughts of my mother consumed me. On the low, I kind of longed for a relationship with her. I guess it was the little girl deep within. But I guess the other side of me (the savage in me) didn't give a fuck. I couldn't beg for something that someone wasn't willing to give. I decided to not even think about it anymore. I closed my eyes and took a well-needed nap.

"Jump on, Mommy." I heard, followed by laughter, which made me wake all the way up. I had my head under the covers still. I decided to mess with them.

"It's not mommy; it's the tickle monster." I joked before I grabbed my baby boy's leg to pull him down. Tickling him, he laughed until I heard him pass gas.

"Ewww!" We all said before we started laughing.

"Bae, take them out for a second. I need to put clothes on." I made it a point to never be naked around my kids. I thought that was so tacky. When they were out the room, I hurried over to the dresser and grabbed a t-shirt and a pair of pajama pants. After slipping them on, I called them back in the room. Of course the boys jumped on the bed. Mahki jumped up and down on the bed while Jr. sat next to me. At four and five, they were so different from each other. Mahki was way more rambunctious where Jr was more quiet and observant. He still enjoyed childlike things; he just was a laid back child.

"What do y'all want for dinner?"

"Pizza!" Mahki yelled out.

"Chicken." Jr answered.

"So how about pizza and wings?" Juelz asked them before I could.

"Yeah. I hope it's plain pizza." Jr added in.

"Of course." Juelz answered him.

"I'll go and order the food." I told them as I got up from the bed.

I grabbed my phone and walked out the room. Looking at the boys made me realize how messed up the relationship with my mother is. As I walked out the room, I could feel Juelz's eyes burning my back. I knew that he was going to question the hell out of me when we were alone. I brushed it off as I walked down the stairs. I walked into the kitchen and grabbed a glass before going to the freezer and grabbing the frozen grapes I had. I poured me a glass of Moscato before dropping the grapes in it. I let it sit while I called and ordered the pizza and wings.

After I was done, I pushed my phone to the side, grabbed my glass, and walked to a quiet place of the house. I was mad that all these thoughts of my mother were in my head. The more thoughts that ran through, the more I drank. I ended up finishing the entire bottle. I went to grab another bottle and my phone too. I didn't feel like going to get my kindle so I just pulled up my kindle app on my phone. Just like Ameerah, my favorite author was Andrea. She was so underrated, but she wrote about real shit. She doesn't go to the extreme on some fantasy shit like others do. Plus, she was from Jersey, too. I was behind on her books, because I'd been busy, so I had to buy the ones that I missed, but first, I had to finish off *Money Can't Keep Me Warm* so I picked up where I left off at.

I was at the part where Brooklyn found out about Tinka. Lord, she should have killed that bitch dead. I didn't play with other bitches when it came to Juelz. He knew what it was and vice versa. I ended up finishing the book while damn near halfway done with the second bottle, and I moved on to the next book. I was deep into it when Juelz came to where I was. He seemed to have an aggravated look on his face. I guess he was mad at me, but I didn't care. The wine had snuck up on me, and I was in a giggly mood.

"Yo, what the fuck is wrong with you?" He barked loud as hell making me jump a little before I started laughing.

"What you talking 'bout?" I was a little confused.

"The way you fucking acting. First, you don't pick the boys up which is not normal. I don't mind picking them up, but you say that's your special time with them. Then, come home and climb right in the bed. The boys here, but you not spending time with them. Then you take it upon yourself to stay down here for damn near an hour and get drunk basically saying fuck the fact that we were upstairs waiting for your ass to fucking come back!" He yelled at me.

48

"SO AGAIN, WHAT THE FUCK IS WRONG WITH YOU? Don't shrug a shoulder or nothing! Open your fucking mouth and let a nigga know what the fuck is going on." He was so close to my face yelling at me, I felt like a child that was getting in trouble. I turned my head away from him. I really didn't feel like talking. He was about to say something when my phone rang. *Saved by the phone.* I thought to myself.

"Hello." I answered, when I saw that it was Ameerah.

"What you doing?" She asked.

"Nothing. Why?" I was curious.

"Just checking on you after earlier today at the mall." She said sincerely.

"I'm fine." I was about to say more when I was cut off. Juelz snatched my phone out of my hand and threw it against the wall. It shattered when it hit the floor.

"That's disrespectful as fuck! Why would you go and start a conversation on the phone, and I'm standing here? You could have told Ameerah that you would call her back." Juelz was really pissed the fuck off. I couldn't do nothing but tell him what was up. He was mad and wasn't going to let up on it. I took a deep breath before explaining everything to him.

"My mom and dad both were on my mind. I went to go and see my mom. Of course that didn't go well at all. I had to just walk away, but not before she told me to watch my back. The way she said it is kind of messing with me on top of her just being as mad as she is."

Andrea

"Fuck that bitch, Miyonna! No fucking body on the planet should fuck with you that bad where it makes you act weirdly towards your kids. They are our first, second, and last priority. Fuck everyone else when it comes to them."

"I know that! I was just sad that I looked at the boys and realized that I give my life, limbs, and all that for them, but my own mother would rather hold a grudge and hate me over something that was super petty."

"I don't know what to say about that Mimi, but what I can say is that, at the end of the day, you got the boys, Ameerah, Monte`, your sister and brother, and me. We love you." He leaned down and kissed my lips. I returned the kiss, but that didn't make feel better. I didn't know why, but I had this nagging feeling that was really bothering me. I wish my father was here.

. . .

It was after three, and I couldn't sleep. For some reason, I had this funny feeling lingering inside of me. I looked over to the side of the bed and saw that Juelz was knocked out without a care in the world. I slid out the bed and headed down the stairs. I walked right to the liquor cabinet and grabbed a bottle of Henny. I was about to get drunk to put myself to sleep. I brought the bottle back upstairs with me. Then, I climbed back in the bed before cracking the bottle. Damn near halfway through the bottle, I was put down.

"Miyonna! Get the fuck up! You don't hear your phone ringing? Then, you smell like them drunks that be posted up on Broadway in front of the liquor store. Clean yourself up. I don't know what your problem is, for real, but you need to fix that shit or let me help you. I mean help you for real, too. Not just tell me pieces of shit and expect me to be psychic."

"Whatever." I mumbled before getting out of bed and walking to the bathroom. I made sure to slam the door behind me and lock it. I didn't plan on going outside, but I was about to go and chill with my niggas. Juelz was touching my nerves already and the day bar was touching my nerves already and the day barely started. I needed to get away from him.

After showering, I threw on my jeans and shirt before walking out the bathroom and into the closet to grab my Timbs and put them on. I grabbed my hoodie and threw it on. Placing my hair in a bun, I grabbed my wallet and keys before heading out my bedroom and down the stairs right out the door. I jumped in my car and pulled off but not before looking up and seeing Juelz in the doorway. I kept on out the driveway, but when I got to the light, I realized that I had left my main phone in the house and only had my burner phone on me. I hurried and texted my little crew and told them to meet me at the spot. My girl Drea texted back and said that she was already there. Pulling up to our chill spot, I saw that everyone's cars was there already. I hopped out and hurried inside.

"Hey Drea." I dapped her up. Drea was the leader of my hit team. She and her girls were official as hell, and I fucked with her the hard way for real.

"Ain't shit. Chilling. Trying to enjoy this little bit of free time I have right now. What you up to?" She asked as I sat down.

"Nothing. I was annoyed so I had to get out the house. I decided to see what y'all was doing."

"We just chilling. You know. I was waiting for the girls to get here and shit."

"Word."

"You good? You look like you're kind of just staring off into space and what not." She looked like she was really concerned.

"Yeah. Girl, I'm fine." I smiled. I thought Drea was cool as hell, but I liked to keep my personal business private.

"Okay, but if you need to talk about anything, just know that I am here. I got you."

"Thank you." I smiled again. I wanted to change the subject and enjoy the rest of the day. It started off bad, but I wanted it to turn out better. I knew Juelz was mad as hell right now, but I would deal with it later.

Chapter 6: Juelz Johnson

I don't know what was going on with Miyonna and her mood swings, but she needed to get them in check. I'm trying to be patient with her, because I know how shit is with her and her mom, but she doing too much with the shutting me out, though.

After she had gone into the bathroom, I headed down the stairs with the boys; they were sitting in the kitchen waiting for us so that we could eat breakfast. I had just sat down when I heard Miyonna running down the steps. I was about to say something when I heard the door open and shut. I made it to the door just in time to see her pulling out. I saw her look up at me, but she still pulled off. I walked away from the door and closed it before going to grab my phone. I called her phone, but hung up when I heard it ringing in the house. She was really doing entirely too much, and I was not about to deal with her attitude, because I'mma end up putting my hands on her.

"Daddy, where is Mommy?" Our baby boy Mahki asked. He was a mama's boy. I ain't really like that shit, but what could I really do?

"She went to work. We will see her later."

"How come we all don't hang together, all of us?" Jr asked, and I didn't know what to say.

"Let's just eat. We will have a men's day today. Okay?" I asked them. Miyonna and I were going to sit down and put everything on the table. She gon' have to open her mouth and talk about shit. Even if she didn't want to, because something was going to have to give.

After getting me and the boys dressed, I decided to take them to iPlay America. I just wanted them to have a good day.

"Hey Juelz, man! What's up?" I heard someone say. We turned around and a little boy came running towards us. He ran over to Jr, and they dapped each other up.

"What's up Marquise? You want to play with us?" He just invited the little boy to play with us. I shook my head to avoid laughing at the look on Mahki's face. He was not trying to share his brother.

"Who this, Jr?" I asked with a chuckle. Mahki was pissed.

"This my friend from school. He can play with me and Mahki."

"I want, Mommy." Mahki started to crack his face up. I looked at him daring him to cry.

"He needs to ask his mom, Jr."

"My mommy is right behind you." He pointed behind me, and I turned around as she was walking near us.

"So this is the infamous Juelz from school, huh?" I looked at the little boy's mom; she had a sweet little voice, but it didn't really match her appearance but whatever.

"Yeah, Mommy. This is my best friend."

"Okay." She just smiled at him.

"Let's go play." I told them, as we moved towards something that was suitable for the kids to play. We all had fun playing at iPlay before the kids started to get irritated. I realized that it was getting dark outside. We got ready to head home when Jr asked if the little boy could come over and spend the night. I wanted to say no, but they both were damn near begging, and I didn't want to do my Jr like that, so I told them yeah.

After the little boy's mom had agreed, we exchanged numbers so I could send her the address and stuff to the house. She kissed her son goodbye, and we headed to the house.

Pulling up to the house, I saw that Ameerah was pulling up as well. When she got out the car, she looked mad as hell.

"You good Ameerah?" I asked her when she hopped out of the car.

"Nah. Where is Miyonna? I been calling her all damn day. That's not like her to be not returning my calls or not answering." She snapped.

"She busy with something. She left her phone home." I let her know.

"How you know?"

"She left before we did this morning." I told her before turning to the boys and telling them to go to the playroom.

"Oh. I was ready to fuck shit up. She just doesn't know!"

"I bet." I smirked.

"Alright. Let me get back to Monte` and Princess. Tell Miyonna to call me when she gets in." She hugged me then headed to the door.

"Word."

I walked her to the door and locked it behind her. I watched until she pulled off before I went and checked on the boys before going back to the living room and taking a sit down. I couldn't say that Miyonna wasn't on my mind, because she was. She was really on some spoiled brat shit right about now. I feel like, if she was this depressed over her mom and her feelings, then maybe she should pass her position down. At the end of the day, her sanity and attitude towards me and our sons were all that mattered to me.

Yeah, Miyonna was thorough to the outside world, but behind it all, she was emotional and got in her feelings quick like every other female. The boys and I were all showered and in bed. I was wide awake as I waited for Mimi to get home. I had already done my Mr. Mom duties. The little boy Marquise's mom had brought him some clothes over so he was showered and in the bed, too. I was confident in myself, and as a man, so I didn't feel like a bitch waiting for my bitch to get home. It was what it was. We were partners in this shit. I heard feet lightly coming up the steps. I looked at the clock just as Miyonna was walking in the room. It was after eleven o'clock.

"Hey bae." She said lightly. She must have been in a good mood.

56

"Wassup? Come sit down real quick. We need to talk about something." I wasn't about to beat around the bush or hold my tongue for shit. After stripping down to her bra and panties, she climbed in the bed with me. She leaned over and kissed me on the lips. That mood swing shit. She was just mad at me this morning.

"What you want to talk about?" She asked.

"I was thinking about something. If you are that fucked up about your mom, maybe you should reconsider your position. Obviously, you are hurt as fuck and want a relationship with her."

"What? I…" She cut me off but I wasn't done yet.

"Let me finish. Like I was saying before you interrupted me, something has to give. Look how you been acting since you went over there. We ain't do shit to you. So acknowledge your mother's wishes and make amends with her or let that shit go and accept the fact that y'all not going to have that close mother/daughter bond." I let her know, plain and simple.

"I knew this shit was going to happen. You must be jealous of my position or just waiting for an opportunity so you could tell me to step down and let it go! Well, I'm not doing it! So fuck you! You sound like a hater, because I'm more thorough than you. Fuck out of here trying to make it seem like I'm doing something to the kids." She yelled as she jumped up out the bed. I got up, too. She had me fucked up.

"Pipe the fuck down! I ain't jealous of shit. Never have and never will be. Let's be honest since you talking shit. If it weren't for your father, you wouldn't even be in the position, and if your older sibling wouldn't have died, you damn sure wouldn't be in the position. So get the fuck on! I'm a thorough ass nigga that worked from the bottom for my shit. Nobody ain't give me shit or pass shit down to me. Remember that before trying to talk that shit to me." She smacked the shit out of me.

"Fuck you, Juelz! Don't you dare bring up my brother. I don't talk about your fucked up fruit cake ass family so don't do mine." She yelled with tears in her eyes.

"Put your hands on me again! I fucking dare you to! Do I fucking hit you? No, I don't hit it!" I was mad as hell.

"Hit me back, Juelz! I fucking dare you, too. I will shoot them bitches off!" She yelled.

"I think you left Miyonna somewhere and brought Pocha home with you, because you trying it right now. I ain't scared of your ass in the streets, and I damn sure ain't scared of your ass right here in this house." I let her know. Shit, she had me on ten right now. I was pissed the fuck off.

"Whatever! I didn't say that you were scared. Plus, there's no fun when the other person is scared." She said, smartly, while looking me right in my eyes. But I knew Miyonna well enough to know that she wanted to bust out crying at any moment.

"You talking real tough right now, Miyonna."

"Oh, whatever. I'm not talking nothing. That's you."

"As your man, I was giving you advice. Your mouth really getting crazy. I'm not these bitch ass niggas. You need to control that shit. Remember who the fuck you talking to." I let her know while glaring at her. She must have felt that I wasn't playing with her ass because she calmed down. I wasn't too fond of her ass at that moment though. I laid back down and turned my back to her. I didn't care if she was mad or not at me for doing that. "Oh yeah, Ameerah said to call her. If you do, I hope you go down the stairs and do that shit."

"I wish you shut up." She mumbled but I heard her. I didn't respond, though. I couldn't respond, cuz it would have escalated then. I am not a woman beater. I closed my eyes just as I heard my phone buzz. I reached to the nightstand and picked it up. I looked at it and saw that it was a blocked number calling me. I was hesitant, but I answered anyway.

"Hello?"

"This Ju, right?" The caller asked.

"You should know since you calling this phone."

"Oh. Yup, it sounds like you. Anyways, tell your boy to stop playing with me." The caller said before laughing then hanging up the phone. I didn't know who that was, but I had an idea. All I could do was shake my head.

Before putting my phone on the charger, I sent a group text to my niggas. Once they all responded, I put my phone on the charger and closed my eyes to let sleep take over me, but that didn't last long when Miyonna came barging in the room with another attitude.

"Who was the bitch that was smiling all in your and my kids' face?" Miyonna was all in my face. I couldn't deny how sexy she was looking.

"What you talking about?" I asked her.

"At iPlay. Stop playing. You know what I'm talking about."

"Oh. Jr's little friend's mom. The little boy is here in the room with Jr." I told her.

"Why that bitch was skinning and grinning? Like, do she know who I am?" Mimi said that, and I fell out laughing. "Stop laughing. I'm serious." I couldn't even take her serious after that shit she said so I just pulled her down in the bed with me. I ripped her panties off of her before running my fingers across her pretty pussy. I smiled as she shuddered. She might piss me off, but my baby was the sexiest bitch on the planet. I leaned in to kiss her while undoing her bra as well. I tossed it to the side before trailing my kisses from her lips down her body until I got to her pussy. I opened her thighs as wide as they would go and dove in head first.

"Shhhhhhh! Ba-bae, I-I'm still on the phone." She stuttered out. I moved my head from in between her legs.

"Tell them goodnight then hang the fuck up!" I told her before my head went back in between her legs. She tried to move her legs, but I held onto them tightly, as I used my tongue to play with her clit. I sucked it in my mouth before

60

letting it out and using the tip of my tongue to tickle it. I knew she was about to cum when she palmed my head.

She gripped it tightly and started to hump my face, and before I knew it, her juices were running down it. I let go of her legs before kissing up her body. I took her phone out her hands and sat it on the nightstand before I lined my dick up at her opening making sure to rub it up and down to make her wetter before sliding in. I was giving her deep strokes, when she put her face in my neck and sucked on it making me pull back. I stopped stroking.

"Why you quiet? Let me hear you."

"Stop playing, bae. Keep going." She whined, as she ground her body against me. I smirked, as I pulled out, and flipped her over, raised her ass up, and pushed her chest down. I rammed my whole dick inside of her and temporarily silenced her.

"Talk to daddy." I smacked her on the ass.

"Fuck! Fuck! Fuck me harder!" She was throwing her ass back at me, but I did what she asked and fucked her harder.

"Cum for daddy!" I reached around and played with her clit, applying pressure to it.

"Papi, I'm 'bout to cum."

"You know what to do." I told her, and before I knew it, her juices were spraying all over me. It was like kryptonite, because I was right behind her. I placed kisses up her back. Once we got ourselves together, we got under the covers. She came close to me and laid her head on my chest. Before long,

I heard light snoring. I kissed her forehead and took my ass to sleep too.

...

I thought I was dreaming when I woke up to some amazing head. I opened my eyes and lifted up the blanket and watched as Miyonna's head bobbed up and down on my dick. My toes curled when she took me deep down her throat. She looked up at me and winked while still doing her thing.

Reaching down and gripping her hair, I got a tight hold of it and started to fuck her mouth. She latched onto my dick tight as hell when I started to cum. She swallowed everything then had the nerve to keep on sucking. I had to yank her by the hair to get her to let go. She let my dick drop from her mouth. Then, kissed up my body to my lips.

"Morning, Papi." She smiled.

"Good morning. You in a good mood, I see."

"Yeah. I want to apologize for last night. I'm going to take your advice and let the shit with my mom go. We obviously aren't going to have the mother/daughter bond, so I'm going to just let it go."

"Alright. So we not going to talk about this anymore? You not going to be acting crazy and shit no more, right?" I asked her. I wasn't going to deal with them mood swings all the time.

"No. I'm good. I promise. I am so sorry. Can we just spend the day together? You, me, and the boys?" She asked me.

"Yeah. Let's go see if they up so that little boy can go home, and we can have a family day." I watched as Miyonna stood up and walked over to the dresser naked. The way her ass jiggled as she walked made me want to lock the bedroom door all day and have her to myself, but I knew that the boys deserved time with her, so I wasn't going to do that.

I watched as she slipped on a pair of my boxers and a t-shirt, then grabbed her robe. I slipped on some basketball shorts and a tank top before we walked in the bathroom and handled our hygiene before walking out the room. When we walked into the boys' room, they were up playing the game.

"Morning babies. Who is this?" Miyonna picked Mahki up when he ran to her. He kissed her all over her face. I just shook my head, because I really needed to break him out of being a mama's boy.

"Mommy, I missed you. That's Jr's friend Marquise." Mahki said, while trying to roll his eyes.

"I missed you. We are going to take Jr's friend home, and then we are going to watch movies and have fun all day. Okay?"

"Yay! Come on, Marquise, so you can go home with your own mommy." Mahki told him. I turned my head and busted out laughing. My son was off the chain.

"Go wash y'all faces while Miyonna goes to cook breakfast. When you done, I will call your mom to come and get you. Okay?"

"Why can't he stay Mommy and Dad?" Jr asked. I just looked at Miyonna.

"We having a family day today. That's why." She put Mahki down then walked away and headed down the stairs. I walked back to my bedroom and grabbed my phone sending a group chat letting my niggas know not to hit me up for nothing.

After the little boy had gone home, we headed to the family room to watch movies. That's basically all we did all day was watch movies, play games, and eat snacks. As long as my babies were good, then so was I. Miyonna cooked dinner for us, and we sat down and had a family dinner. All in all, it was a good day.

The next day, it was back to the grind, but first, I had to stop and see my mom and grandma. When my grandma got sick, my mom moved her in with her. I didn't mind that that, though. I loved them both to death. When I pulled up to the house, I saw that there was another car in the driveway, so I hurried inside to see who was at my mother's house. I walked in and followed the direction of the arguing voices. I walked into the kitchen, and it was my mom and brother arguing.

"What's going on?"

"I'm asking her why she ignoring pops, man. She gon' tell me to mind my business. How she gon' be the adult but acting childish?" My little brother Jamar wanted everyone to get along, but I didn't blame my mom for not wanting to be at that point yet. I mean, my pops did cheat on her with a man.

She was blindsided with that shit, so of course she not going to be so all open-armed. I personally didn't care who he lived with or loved; I just didn't like how he did my mother.

"Chill out, man. Don't be coming for mom like that. Back up out her face like that."

"Alright. Sorry, Ma. We supposed to be family, but we not acting like one. Things need to get better." Jamar said, and I didn't say anything back. He was nineteen and was spoiled as hell. He turned and looked at me. "Juelz, Pops been wanting you to call him. He said that he wants to talk to you about something."

"I'm not calling him, Mar. Sorry, but nah." I let him know.

"So y'all really turning y'all back on pops when we all supposed to stick together. Then, on top of that, it's been a few years. Everyone need to let it go. Daddy happy in love with Jack. We need to support him."

"Jamar, I'm not at the place to be extra friendly. To be honest, I honestly don't care about what your father is doing. He cheated on me, and I am not that forgiving about that. Then, to top it off, it was with a man. That just adds embarrassment to the hurt, so no thank you with the happy family scenario."

"But, Ma…"

"End of discussion, Jamar." My mom shut it down. I laughed at her, and he got mad instantly.

"I'm out." He grabbed his keys and headed out the door. I waited until I heard the door close before I fell out laughing. He was really mad as hell.

"He really mad, huh, Ma? So how did that even start?" I asked her.

"James been calling me, but I was ignoring him before I ended up putting him on the block list. I will deal with him when I feel like I want to. If you want to call him, go ahead. I won't love you any less, and I would understand."

"Nah, Mom. I'm good. Anyway, I just came here to check on you. I wanted to talk to you about something, but it's been enough going on. I will call you later." I kissed her on the cheek before heading towards the door; I didn't want to give her a chance to say anything. I had wanted a female's point of view of this shit with Miyonna, but it was enough going on, so I just decided to wait. I jumped in my car and sped off.

...

"What y'all in here doing?" I asked, when I walked into the trap. I went around the room dapping everyone up before sitting down.

"Shit. Was waiting for everyone to come through, so I could talk to everyone at once." The man looked down at his phone. "I texted everyone. They should be on their way."

"Alright." I pulled my phone out and saw that I had a text message. When I opened it, I almost dropped my phone. Miyonna sent me a perfect view of her pussy. That shit was so pretty, and I can tell that she was playing with it, because it had a glisten to it. My dick shot up. I looked around to make sure no one was looking at me.

"You good, Big Homie?" Man asked.

"Y-yeah. I'm straight." I tried to sound normal.

"You sure?"

"Yeah." I told him before texting Miyonna to see if she was going to be home in about an hour. When she said that she was going to meet me there, that's all I had to hear. Now I was ready for Man to say what he had to say so I could go meet my baby at the house.

Ten minutes later, everyone was here, and Man had the floor. He looked at me and sighed deeply. I don't know why, but I felt that he was about to say some personal shit. I just braced myself and waited.

"So I got Bam at the spot and shit. He tied up, and his ass started talking shit. Saying he took the money, cuz he deserved it. I'm not going to beat around the bush, but he mumbled something about killing Miyonna to teach you a lesson. I punched his teeth out, but I'mma let you handle him. He might have more to say if he sees your face."

"Word. Let's head to the spot. I don't want to hear shit else. Let's go! This nigga fucking wiling." We all jumped up and headed to the warehouse where we did dirt at. I didn't want no one riding with me over there, because I was in deep thought. I knew that Miyonna could handle herself, but I also knew that, if she was with the kids, then she wasn't strapped. I was gon' figure all of this shit out.

Andrea

We pulled up at the same time and jumped out. I walked right to where that nigga Bam was. His eyes were closed like he was napping, and I heard breathing so I knew that he wasn't dead. I picked up a steel bat that was on the floor and swung it, hitting his face. That woke his ass up.

"The fuck!" He groaned.

"Wake the fuck up! I heard you were talking greasy bout a nigga. I'm here now! What's up?" I stood in front of him.

"Kill me witcho bitch ass. I said all I had to say." He was talking a lot of shit. I liked that, though. It showed that he had a little bit of heart in him. He was still going to die, though; that was inevitable.

"Who you working with? You ain't got the brains to do this by yourself?" I said to him.

"I ain't no snitch, but what I will say is that it's somebody that don't like you or your bitch. Now, kill me! I ain't snitching and saying a name, bitch." He got smart. I turned and looked at my niggas to make sure they were hearing what I was hearing. They nodded that they understood, and I just shook my head.

"Man, fuck this." I grabbed the machete that was laid on the floor and took that nigga head off. We kept a lot of weapons and shit laid around the warehouse at our disposal. I felt like we did enough talking, and he wasn't going to say anything else, so it was what it was. I dropped the head in a garbage bag before looking at my niggas again, and they looked shocked as hell.

"Put this in the freezer so that, when we find the mothafucka that he was working with, we can set the head on the doorstep. Let them know loud and clear what happens when you fuck with us, feel me?"

"Word." Man said to me. I noticed that Monte` was quiet as hell as he stood off to the side texting away on his phone. I walked to the back where the bathroom was and washed my hands before coming back out, and he was still deep in his phone.

"Yo, Mont!" I called him to get his attention. He looked at me, but the look in his eyes was weird, like his thoughts were somewhere else. "Yo, you good? I'm about to be out. 'Bout to hit the crib real quick before I check on the block boys."

"That's what's up. I gotta handle some personal shit then head to the crib. I'll get up with you later." He dapped me up, and we both headed out to our cars. He was still deep in his phone when I hopped in my car and pulled off. I hoped my nigga wasn't cheating again. That was something I wasn't trying to go through, though, because he and Ameerah's business became mine and Miyonna's. I hated being in other people's bullshit or business.

When I got to the house, I hurried inside and ran all the way up the stairs. I was taken back when I walked in, and Miyonna was laid across our bed in some sexy lingerie. She was about to be crushed. Sex had to wait for a second.

"Bae, we need to talk."

Chapter 7: Ameerah Statum

I was at work all day showing houses, condos, townhouses, etc. This was one of my busier days, and I swear I couldn't wait to get home, take a nice, hot shower, and stretch out on the bed while I wait for my baby to get home so I could get some head and dick. Then, I would be put right to sleep. Thank God, I only have one more day of the week to work, then I will be home for a few days getting my house together.

I was on my way to show my last house for the day. It was after five in the afternoon, and my ass was tired as hell, but I wasn't about to let it show. I was going to do what I do best and be the savage real estate agent that I was. I ended up getting to the property before my client did so I did a quick walkthrough while I waited. I walked back to the front of the house when I heard a car pull up. It was a white Escalade, and when the door opened, and this fine ass man hopped out, I had to fan myself to make sure I wasn't dreaming. I closed my eyes and thought about my baby's dick game. That brought me right back to reality.

"Ms. Statum?" The guy asked. I nodded.

"Mr. Marks?" I asked him.

"That's me."

A Lady in the Sheets, A Savage in the Streets

"Okay. You can follow me." We walked into the house, and I stopped near the doorway. "So this house is a five bedroom, three-and-a-half-bath."

"What is the asking price?" He was staring at me intently.

"The asking price is four-fifty. It has a four-car garage as you can see when you pulled up. If you continue to follow me, we can go and see the rest of the house." We walked through to the kitchen after the living room. "So this kitchen is fully remodeled. From the stainless steel counters, a new floor, and state-of-the-art stove."

"Everything in the kitchen is new?"

"Yes, sir. Shall we keep on?" I asked, as I led the way, making small talk about the steps as we neared them. We headed to the master bedroom first. "This is the master bedroom. It has a walk-in closet, a full bathroom, and a lot of space. Any questions?"

"Yes. I have one…" He smiled at me with a weird smile. "Do you think the closet is big enough for you to put your stuff in?"

"Excuse me!" I was taken back by his ass.

"What I'm trying to say is that you should be my woman…" My phone rang, and I grabbed it to silence it. Well, that was until I saw that it was my daughter's school calling.

"Can you excuse me? It's my daughter's school." I walked into the hallway and answered the phone.

"Hello?" I answered.

Andrea

"Hello, Ms. Statum. This is Miss Tower from Kidde Learning Center. I am calling you, because your daughter Princess Washington wasn't picked up yet, and it is getting late. School ended about three hours ago. I sent her to the aftercare program, but that just ended for the day and still no one is here to pick her up."

"Oh my god. I am at work right now, but I am on my way. I will be there in the next fifteen minutes." I was so mad at Mont's ass. He knew that he was supposed to pick her up. What the fuck was he doing that was more important than our child?

"Okay. That would be nice, but this cannot happen every day."

"It won't. I will be there soon." I said before hanging up. I walked back in the room with my client. He looked at me like he knew something was wrong.

"Is everything okay?"

"No. I have to reschedule you for another day. I have an emergency. I will have my assistant get in touch with you. See you later." I rushed down the stairs and out the door to my car. I felt him behind me, but I didn't even care. I walked over to my car and frowned my face when I saw that there was a note on my windshield. I snatched it off and hopped in my car. Starting it up, I pulled off. When I got to the light, I opened the letter and read it.

Tell our nigga that I'm not playing with him.

Now, somebody was playing and shit. Who the fuck does shit like this, I really didn't know. I tried calling Mont's ass over and over, but his ass was sending me to voicemail. I politely left his ass a nice message.

"I don't know what the fuck your black ass is doing, but I know damn well that it's not more important than our fucking daughter. I hope you stay wherever the hell you at, because if you come to the house where me and my daughter at, you going to be in for a rude awakening. Good fucking bye!" I yelled into the phone before hanging up.

People swore that I turn up on his ass for no reason, but it's because of the dumb shit that he does. This was the ultimate hell no! Forgetting about our daughter is the worst. There should be nothing more important than your child. I kept on trying to call him, but his ass still wasn't answering.

Pulling up to the school almost fifteen minutes later, I left the car running while I ran inside. I walked in, and they had Princess sitting in the director's office. I just simply shook my head. This nigga was going to feel me.

"Thank you! This won't happen again." I said, as I picked Princess up.

"I understand that you and your husband both work, but you have to think about your child. I'm being understanding, because this was the first time that this happened."

"Like I said, it won't happen again. She will not be in school tomorrow. You have a nice night." I walked out the office. When we got to the car, I strapped her in her seat and headed home. I tried calling Mont's ass two more times, and just like before, he sent me to voicemail. I called Miyonna, because I needed to vent to her, and I knew that she wouldn't be biased.

"Hello?" She answered, sounding like she was stressed out.

"I'm so fucking mad. So why did Mont leave Princess at school? They called me, and I just picked her up, so I'm calling him like hella times, and he sending my ass to voicemail. If he cheating again, I'm out. Now his bullshit is affecting our child. He leaving her at school as if they don't have the ability to call DYFYS. I really don't know what the fuck is going through his mind."

"Wait-a-minute! You have Princess?"

"Yes. I just picked her up."

"It's like six o'clock. The hell he at?" She asked like I knew.

"I don't know, Mimi. I been calling, and he is not answering. Like, what the fuck!" I snapped.

"Damn. Let me ask Juelz if he knows where he is. Hold on." I heard her in the background talking before I heard shifting around. Then, Juelz hopped on the phone.

"Sis, when I saw him earlier he was acting weird as hell. He said that he had to go handle some personal shit then he was heading home. I ain't heard from or saw him since. I been calling his ass, too, and he ain't answering. I thought his ass was with you so I didn't push. I'm 'bout to go look for his ass, though."

A Lady in the Sheets, A Savage in the Streets

"Thanks, bro. I'm headed home now, so let me know. If he there when I get there, I'll text Mimi phone and let her know." I told him before hanging up. I was now worried. For him to not answer for Juelz, it had to be something serious. They were tight as hell. When Mont cheated, Juelz had his back through it all. I couldn't be mad, because they were niggas.

When I got to the house, I saw that his car wasn't in the driveway at all. I got Princess out, and we walked into the house. She ran off through the house while I sat my purse on the couch and walked into the kitchen. I washed my hands and started to cook while I continuously tried calling Mont, but his ass still wasn't answering the phone. I decided to wait a little bit before calling him back and finished cooking dinner, then called Princess downstairs so that we could eat. I was quiet at dinner racking my brain trying to figure out where Monte was.

"Mommy, where is, Daddy?" Princess asked as she ate her food.

"He is at work. He will be here later." I hated lying to her, but I wasn't about to have her bugging out.

"Okay." was all she said before she went back to eating. She didn't say anything else as she finished her food. I didn't really have an appetite so I got up and made Monte's plate and put the rest away. I waited for Princess to finish eating, then we headed upstairs. After bathing her, I headed to my room. I used the house phone to call Monte's phone. This time, it rang a few times before going to voicemail. Something clicked in my head, and I used the family tracker to see where he was.

When I pulled it up, it showed that his ass was at our house. I jumped up and headed to the window. He was parked in the driveway. I sat my ass on the edge of the bed and waited for him to come in the house. Forgetting that I told Juelz that I would text them, I grabbed my phone and sent a text to Miyonna's phone.

Me: He just got home. I'll talk to y'all tomorrow.

Mimi: Alright. Love you. Don't do nothing crazy. I don't want to be coming over all late and shit. Plus, Juelz ain't here. Ain't nobody got time for that.

Me: lol okay. Love you, too

I sat my phone on the side of me, then lowered my head and looked to the floor. I didn't know what to think. This nigga wasn't answering my calls for hours, was acting funny, and the biggest thing of all, he forgets our daughter at school. I don't know what the fuck is going on, but he needs to fix that shit quick. I was about to get up and walk to the window to see if he was still in the driveway when I heard footsteps coming up the stairs.

"What's good, bae?" This nigga had the nerve to ask, as he walked over to me and kissed me on the side of the head. I moved my head and looked as he acted as if everything was okay.

"Where the fuck you been all day? You didn't see the missed calls?" I asked him with my arms folded against my chest.

"I was busy working."

"Hmmm. Working? So work's more important than our child? So important that you fucking left her at school three hours after school ended? So again, WHERE THE FUCK YOU BEEN ALL DAY?" I stood up and was trying to be face to face with him. I wanted him to see that I was not playing with him.

"Get the fuck out of my face! You doing too much. Respect me as your fucking man! Back the fuck up before I smack the shit out of you." He yelled before slightly pushing me back. I stumbled back into the bed hitting my foot, but I ain't about the pain at the moment.

"Respect you as my man? Really? What about respecting me as your woman and the mother of your child? If that was me, you would have a fucking fit. You got a fucking nerve to be here trying to bark on me and pushing me but you were the one missing all day and left our goddamn child at school. If you were with a bitch, why don't you just go and be with her ass? Why do you do foolishness? Ain't shit more important than my child? Huh?" I asked him.

"I told you to back up. You going to stop coming at me like you don't know who I am. You really feeling yourself right now!"

"I ain't feeling shit. Well, I ain't feeling the way you did our child. All I want to know is what was more important than our child. Let me know."

"Like I said, I was busy working!" He tried to walk off, but I pulled him by his shirt.

"I heard you when you said that, but we both know that is a lie. Juelz was looking for your ass, too. So I think you need to come better than that."

"Get the fuck off of me. Let's get this straight. I'm the man. I wear the fucking pants in the relationship. You follow my lead. Now, like I said, I was busy working."

"Man, fuck you! You weren't working shit but your dick…" I was ready to go the fuck off, but that was short-lived when he grabbed me by my neck and squeezed slightly.

"Fuck who? Say that shit again where I can hear you." He told me through gritted teeth. I tried to repeat what I said, and he squeezed tighter cutting off my air circulation. I chose to be quiet, then he let up and let go of me. I backed up and rubbed my neck before I said anything else.

"Like I said, fuck you, and the weak shit that you saying." I walked backward towards the door, but something clicked in my head making me stop. I looked at him with pure disgust. "So what race is this bitch? Spanish? A thick, white bitch? She from the Islands? Shit, let me know. You had most ethnicities already."

"Shut the fuck up, Ameerah."

"Nope. I'm not ever going to shut up! You really put a bitch before my child. I'm always gon' run my mouth every time I see your ass."

"The fuck is you talking about? We live together. You see me every day." He said, and I rolled my eyes.

"No we don't! You can get the fuck out. Go be with them bum bitches. It's sad that you fuck with all these bitches that if you build them up, they still wouldn't be half the bitch that I am. So fuck you and get out!" I said, before picking up my phone and walking out the room. I walked to Princess' room. I knew that he wouldn't do too much in front of her. Like I knew he would, he followed right behind me.

"I really don't know why you following me. Get the fuck out. I'm sick of your shit. I swear to God I am. Stupid of me to fall for your lies. The ones where, when you swore on Princess that you not cheating no more. Remember you said that was old and that was years ago. You said that you ain't cheated since I left you some years back. Remember that bitch ass nigga! I guess that right there should have told me that you don't give a fuck about her. So you can go. Get out!" Princess jumped right into my arms and hugged me tight. I felt bad that she was crying. "Shh! Stop crying baby. Mommy is sorry for yelling in front of you."

"Why the fuck would you bring your dumbass in her room with the bullshit?"

"Why you acting like you care when you know that you don't? If you get out, I won't say shit else." I told him as I texted Mimi for her to tell Juclz to come and get him. I really didn't want to look at his lying ass right now. I was glad when she texted back that he was on his way.

"Shut the fuck up!"

"You shut up! I wish you weren't her father, then she wouldn't have a clown as a father."

"The fuck you just say to me?" He moved in close. I didn't care that I hit a nerve. "You wish that shit for real? It must have been other possibilities." He snatched Princess out of my arms scaring the shit out of her. He kissed her forehead before laying her in her bed and apologizing. I rolled my eyes, and before I knew it, I was being snatched up by my arm and drug from Princess' room.

"Get the fuck off of me!" I swung my other hand with a closed fist, punching his ass making them hits land any and everywhere. "Get off! Why don't you just leave?"

"I ain't going nowhere! I pay the muthafucking bills in this bitch!" He yelled. I kicked my foot up and hit him in the dick making him let go of my arm. I hit the floor, but I didn't even care. I pounced on him and let all my frustrations out. I was swinging and hitting him wherever my fists landed. I had to get all my hits in, because I knew that, once he got himself together, he was going to grab my ass up. I kept on punching and kicking him until he grabbed my leg which made us roll down the steps.

"Bitch ass nigga grabbing on me." He reached down and smacked the shit out of me. I was shocked, because that was the first time he put his hands on me.

"Now chill the fuck out like I said."

"You really gon' smack me! Word, I got you." I kicked my feet until he let me go. Then, I ran to the kitchen and grabbed the butcher knife. I ran back swinging the knife. He tried to grab it but wasn't quick enough. I ended up stabbing him in the arm right down to the white meat. He reached again but still wasn't quick enough and the knife scratched him across the chest. I lifted the knife up like I was going to stab him in the chest. "Get out before your chest is next. This time it will be on purpose." I told him.

"Yo sis, chill." Juelz walked in with Miyonna. He walked over to me, but I jumped back.

"I'm not chilling until you take your boy and leave." I let him know.

"Meerah, look at him. He is getting weak, and there is a puddle of blood under him."

"Well, y'all should take his ass to the hospital instead of telling me to do something. Right!" I still had the knife up. I wasn't taking any chances at all. Juelz walked Mont out the house, and Miyonna stayed back to try and talk to me, but I didn't have shit to say to her or anyone else. I guess she got the picture, because she walked out, too. When they left, I locked the door then went back to the kitchen and dropped the knife in the sink to run water on it while I went to clean up the blood puddle. I know people probably think that I overreacted, but I don't think I did, because them people could have called child services. Then, that would be a huge investigation on us that we really didn't need. Especially not with that nigga's line of work.

After I was done downstairs, I headed upstairs to Princess' room. I grabbed her some clothes out her dresser and quickly dressed and packed the rest before swooping her up. I was glad that she was sleep. I walked into my room and laid her across my bed as I grabbed some clothes for myself and my laptop. Balancing everything in my hands, I headed down the stairs and out the house.

. . .

Knock. Knock. Knock. I knocked on my mother's door waiting for her to answer. I knew that, when they released Mont's ass from the hospital, he was going to come back to the house, but it was gon' be a surprise when we weren't there. I was about to sit all my stuff on the ground and look for my keys when the door finally opened.

"Hey, baby girl." My mom's husband Melvin said when he opened the door. He was the only father figure that I knew. Him and my mother been married since I was in my teenage years. She always said that she would wait until I was old enough for her to date. I was okay with it. He wasn't fucked up. He didn't treat my mom bad. He treated Princess like she was his biological grandchild, so I didn't mind.

"Hey. Help me."

"I got it. Take Princess, and go lay her down. I'll bring the stuff to the room for you." I was walking to the back of the house when my mom came out the room.

"What you doing here?"

"I will tell the both of y'all after I lay her down." I took her shoes and pants off before putting her under the covers. Melvin walked in behind me with the bags and sat them on the floor before walking out. After making sure Princess couldn't fall out the bed, I walked towards the living room. My mom and Melvin were both sitting on the couch waiting for me. I sat on the recliner across from them.

"So what happened?" My mom asked. I ran everything down to her and watched the shocked expression go across her face as I talked. My mom was shocked, because I usually didn't tell her the details of the shit that goes on in my relationship. I usually kept everything to myself besides the little bit that I told to Miyonna. When I was done, they both were just looking at me.

"I can't believe you stabbed him, Ameerah." Melvin said to me.

"It wasn't really on purpose. I was trying to get him to leave. He went to grab the knife, and I stabbed him." I left out the part about him smacking me because Melvin would try and press him then could possibly end up dead. I ain't want that on my conscience.

"Are you and him over?"

"I really think so, Ma. I'm not going to deal with the cheating again, and he obviously doesn't care about me or Princess or else he wouldn't have forgotten about her today."

"Maybe he was really busy. You don't know."

"Really, Ma? Well, if that's the case, then why was Juelz looking for him, too, and they work together? Huh?" I asked her, and she looked like a deer caught in headlights.

"You just don't know." She just had to throw that in there. I guess you could really tell that my mom was team Monte`.

"Whatever, Ma. You just don't know. I'm about to go and lay down. It's been a long day." I stood up and hugged the both of them before heading back to the room. I grabbed my phone and looked at the time. I saw that it was only a little after nine and that I had missed calls and a few voicemails. I knew it was either Juelz or Miyonna, but I would just talk to them in the morning.

Chapter 8: Monte Washington

Waking up, I was in a lot of pain, and I wasn't exactly sure where I was. I looked around and realized that I was at the hospital. The only question now was, how did I get here? I tried to lift my left arm, but it hurt beyond belief so I lifted the other one to push the call button. A few seconds later, the nurse came walking in.

"How can I help you, Mr. Washington?" She asked, as she started checking my vitals.

"How long have I been here and what happened?" I asked her as she looked me over.

"You came in last night, and you blacked out from losing so much blood after being stabbed. The police are coming back to question you."

"I don't remember shit." I told her which wasn't a lie. I don't remember much from the night before excepting smoking my life away then heading home and smoking some more in the driveway. Everything after that was fuzzy.

"I understand, but that's protocol for them to come. The doctor will be in soon to talk to you." The nurse said before she walked out. I closed my eyes to rest them, and all I could think about was where Ameerah was. The longer I laid there quietly, the more shit started to come back to me. The fight that Ameerah and I had was playing in my head. I never hit her before for real. I roughed her up a few times, but as far as actually slapping her, that was the first time. I was mad as hell that I even did that. The personal shit that I had going on was stressing me out, and I let my anger get the best of me and took that shit out on her. I needed to talk to her, but I didn't know where my shit was. I sighed deeply with my eyes still closed when I felt someone's presence in the room with me. I opened my eyes and there stood Juelz. He was looking like he was concerned and shit. He walked over and dapped me up before sitting in the chair that was near the bed.

"What's good?" I asked him.

"Ain't shit. You good? Ya ass having black-outs and passing out and shit. Had a nigga scared that you were about to check out on us and shit." Juelz was being dead ass serious, and I appreciated that he cared.

"I'm cool."

"Man, what the fuck happened with you and Ameerah last night, bruh? She texted us to come and get you, then when we get there, we see her ass poking ya ass up. The fuck going on?"

"She thinks I'm doing dirt again. I left Princess at school late, but that was my bad. Time really did slip from a nigga. Anyways, she started running her mouth and was punching and kicking me. My reflexes got the best of me, and I back-handed her. Shit went too far last night."

"It sure did. Ameerah not talking to nobody, and we don't know where she at. We called her from both of our phones last night after we left here, but she ain't answer or call us back." He said, and I shook my head. "I know I said a lot to you being that you laid up, but you know how I do. I rather lay it all on the table and let it all sting at once so it can all heal at once. Feel me?"

"Yeah. I feel you. I ain't tripping off that. I'm just worried about her and my daughter. I don't like not knowing where they at. Ay, when you leave here, can you go hit up Fred? See if he can see where she at and if he gets a location, can you pull up and tell her to bring Princess and come to see me?"

"I got you. On another note, keep it a stack with me. You cheating again?"

"Hell, nah! I meant that shit when I said that I wasn't doing that shit no more." I was serious. I haven't cheated since a long time ago.

"Well, what the fuck do you be doing that got her thinking that shit?" He seemed really interested.

"I can't tell you that. It's something that I'm not ready to deal with yet." I wasn't ready for my shit to fall out yet. Juelz was my nigga since the sandbox, but if he couldn't respect my shit, then fuck 'em.

"Alright. Say less my nigga." He reached over and dapped me up with my good arm.

"The nurse said that the doctor should be in here soon. The pigs, too."

"You already know how the pigs do."

"Yeah," was all I said as the doctor came walking in.

Andrea

"Hello, Mr. Washington. How you feeling? I'm Dr. Warner."

"I'm cool. How come I haven't been discharged yet?" I asked. Shit, I was ready to go.

"This is your first time waking up since you came in. You passed out. There was no way that you were going to be discharged then. I was looking at your chart here from the vitals the nurse took, and your blood pressure is slightly high. We need to get that down before you go, so you probably won't be discharged until tomorrow." He looked up at me. "Your emergency contact on your papers is an Ameerah Statum, but she didn't answer, so I left a message for her to call back."

"Oh." I didn't know what else to say.

"Relax, so I can check the wound out." He said before going over to the sink to wash his hands before slipping some gloves on. I watched him as he checked my arm out. It didn't look too bad from where I was looking, but I guess that was a good thing. "It doesn't look bad at all. Your stitches are perfect. Before you are discharged tomorrow, we will tell you how to care for the wound when you are home. For now, are you in pain?"

"Yeah."

"Okay. We will have something administered through your IV. It will probably make you drowsy. The nurse will be right in." He said, before washing his hands again and walking out the room.

88

"I'm 'bout to head out and check on the homies. Then, I'mma go and handle that for you. I'll probably be back later on tonight. You know Mimi gon' be with me."

"I already know." We dapped each other up, and he walked out as the nurse was walking in.

"I got your pain meds for you. Let me scan your wrist bracelet, then I will administer them." She grabbed my right arm and used the scanner. Next thing I knew, she was shooting morphine in my IV. A few minutes later, I was knocked out.

Hours later, I woke up to Juelz's mom sitting in the corner. She was like a second mom to me, so I knew that she would eventually make her way here to see me. When she saw that I was up, she came closer to me. She was about to say something to me when there was a knock on the door. The nurse came in followed by the pigs, and I didn't want to talk to them.

"Mr. Washington, how you feeling?" One of the officers asked.

"I'm good. What can I help you with?" I asked them so that they can hurry and leave.

"Do you remember who attacked you?" The other officer asked.

"I don't remember too much from last night. All I know is that I woke up here." I was lying, but oh well, because I would never snitch Ameerah out.

"You don't remember anything from last night? That's some bullshit. Don't bullshit me!" the first pig chimed in. I guess they were playing good cop, bad cop. This was the bad cop's round.

"He said that he didn't remember anything. Now, if he did, why the fuck would he tell y'all? Ain't like y'all going to do anything to help him. To y'all, he ain't nothing but another nigga that got stabbed or shot. So get the fuck out before we call our lawyer and sue y'all asses. Leave us alone, and go on somewhere about your business." Ma chimed in.

"That's why y'all niggers be popping up dead now. Thinking y'all above the law. I will make sure to attend your funeral and sign the guest book." The one officer said while leaving his card. The other officer left his, too. "If you want us to find the person that stabbed you, here is my card." They turned and walked out the room. I glared at his back. He was going to eat them words, he spoke.

"Don't even, Ma." I said when she was about to say something. "I will handle it." She nodded.

"So what really happened?" She asked, as she pulled a chair up.

"Meerah did it." I told her before going on to explain the story to her. When I was done, she just simply shook her head. She never said too much about Ameerah and my blow-ups since the first one we ever had. I guess she came to the realization that, at the end of the day, we were gon' be together.

"I have nothing to say about this. What are the doctors saying about everything?"

"I haven't been discharged, because the nurse said my blood pressure was high as hell. The doctor said that, in the morning, I should be able to go home."

"Okay. Well, that's good."

We sat talking for a little while longer before she left. I started looking through the room for my shit, and I was glad when I opened the closet and there was a bag in there with my stuff in it. I grabbed the bag and walked back to the bed. My arm was starting to hurt like hell, but I was about to suffer through the pain.

Turning my phone on, I saw that it didn't have a full battery, but oh well. I called Ameerah a few times, and of course, it went to voicemail. I left her a message. I called her a few more times before deciding to call her mom. When her mom said that Ameerah was there, I asked her if she could bring them to the hospital. After she had agreed, she hung up. I pushed my phone to the side about to get back under the covers when someone walked in the room.

"Oh my gosh! We were so worried about you. You okay?" I just stared at the person standing in front of me.

"What the fuck are you even doing here?" I asked them. I slowly leaned up. I was staring at them hard as hell.

"I-we were calling you, and you weren't answering the phone. I called the police station and all the hospitals to see if they had a record, and I finally found you. What happened?"

"I was stabbed, but don't worry about it ,and don't worry about me!" I was getting mad as hell.

"What you mean? You talking crazy as hell."

Man…" I started to say, but was cut off.

"What the fuck is this?" Ameerah walked in the room with her purse looking around. Even though she was looking mad as hell, she was still sexy and looking extra thick in her jeans that was hugging her curves. I felt my dick rocking up. "Who is this?"

"Baby, she…"

"So you call my mother's phone for her to tell me to come see you, and I get here, and it's some random ass bitch here. Wait a minute, I know this bitch. She is one of your hoes from back in the day. This the hoe who ass I beat with that golf club. She must want more; that's why she bringing her hood booger ass up here." Ameerah sat her purse down, and I was praying that she didn't pop the poor girl.

"Who you talking to like that?" The bitch spoke up. Lord, why did she do that?

"I'm talking to him. Stay in your lane over there."

"Bitch…"

"Shut the fuck up! Like I said, that's all me. From the top of his head, to the bottom of his feet, and all in between. So, I'm going to talk to him anyway that I feel like it. Okay, now you can go home girl."

"I'm not going anywhere."

A Lady in the Sheets, A Savage in the Streets

"I wish both of y'all cut it out. Sharanika, get out! Ameerah, calm down!"

"Nope!" They said in unison. Ameerah walked towards me by the bed. She lifted her hand and hit the call button.

"Bitch, you getting out one way or another. Let me show you wifey privileges." She said, as the nurse was walking in.

"How can I help you, Mr. Washington?" The nurse asked.

"I'm going to go. I will see you later." Sharanika said, as she walked out the room.

"Hello, I'm his wife, and I wanted to get the rundown of everything. Can you bring a doctor in here so I can talk to you both?" Ameerah did a phony ass smile. That was one thing I liked about her. No matter what she was going through, she never let it show to strangers. She kept it together. At the same time, I was shocked that she even argued with the hood rat like she did before calling the nurse in the room. I guess she was really mad and lost it for a minute before coming back to reality. The nurse nodded before walking out. When she was fully out the room, Ameerah looked at me before punching me hard as hell in the chest before slapping down on my stitched-up arm as hard as she could.

"Ahhhhhhhh! Fucking Bitch!" I snapped.

"Your mother! Now why the fuck was that bitch here?"

"She my baby mother." I said letting it slip out.

...

It's been a few weeks since the night at the hospital, and I haven't seen or spoken to Ameerah at all. She not talking to me at all. She doesn't go over Juelz and Miyonna's house, because she not talking to Juelz, either. I guess she feels like Juelz knew about Sharanika and was smiling in her face. I really don't know, cuz she ain't talking to me.

After I let it slip at the hospital about Sharanika, Ameerah waited for the doctor to come and tell her everything. Then, after he left, she did too. She didn't even care that she had my arm bleeding again. That shit had hurt like a bitch, too. I thugged it out, though. I ended up having to stay an extra day, because of the swelling and my pressure not going down, but a nigga was good now. Thank God they gave me the dissolvable stitches, because I wasn't trying to go back to get them taken out. That was weeks ago, and a nigga was good now.

"Daddy, can we go get Mommy and go to R-Bounce?" Princess asked from the backseat. It was my time to spend with her, and I was about to take her shopping at Toys "R" Us before taking her out to eat.

"Next time, my Princess. Today is just our day together." I looked through the rearview mirror and told her.

"Okay, Daddy. I want Skye from the Paw Patrol. I miss Kerro, too, Daddy. Am I staying at your house?"

"My house? That's your house, too."

"Not uh! Mommy said that we moving to a new house after they finish fixing it. Just me and her and you live at the old house with Kerro."

"No that's still you and Mommy's house, too."

"So why come we live with Ma-Ma then?" She asked in her little voice.

"Only for a little bit then y'all coming back home. Okay, Princess?"

"Yes, Daddy."

"I love you, Princess. Now, you ready to have fun at Toys "R" Us?"

"Yayyyyy! Yes, Daddy. I love you, too. I'm ready."

When we got to the store, I followed behind Princess with a cart as she ran around the store grabbing any and everything she could. As long as she was happy, so was I. We ended up having dinner at Applebee's, which was her request. When we sat down and ordered our food, I wanted to talk to her about something.

"Hey, Princess, what if I told you that you have a big brother?" I asked her, and her eyes lit up.

"Yay! I'm happy. So where he at?" She looked around making me laugh.

"He at home. We going to see him after dinner." I told her, and she was excited. My son, Prince, that I had with Sharanika is a few months older than Princess. After we were done with our food, we headed to Sharanika's house, and I said a prayer all the way over there. Sharanika made me want to wring her neck most of the time, so I said a prayer that everything went smoothly when we got there. I knew that Ameerah would shit a brick if she knew that I was taking our daughter over there, but I really didn't care, because there was

95

no way that my kids were going to grow up not knowing each other.

When I pulled up to Sharanika's house, I grabbed my Desert Eagle and slipped it in my pocket. Shit, she lived in the hood, and there was no way I was going to be caught slipping if something popped off.

Chapter 9: Juelz Johnson

It has been a lot going on in the last few weeks. From Ameerah and her issues with everyone, including me, to me and my niggas still looking for the person that Bam was working with that was talking about killing Miyonna. I felt like I was in a Twilight Zone, but I was taking a break from it all and taking a vacation with all three of my babies and the kids' nanny.

Miyonna wanted it to be a baecation, but I said that we should just bring the boys. That way, we could enjoy our time and not worry about calling constantly to check on them. I didn't tell her what Bam said, because I was going to handle everything before it even became a big issue. We decided to go to Puerto Rico, and I was just glad to spend some time with my family.

As soon as our flight landed, we walked out of the airport into nice, warm weather. I was feeling a slight relaxation right there. I guess Miyonna was, too.

"Thank you so much, bae. I guess I really needed this vacation, too." Mimi kissed me on the lips. She and the kids' nanny grabbed both of our sons' hands and walked towards the rental car that we had. I got the bags in the car then headed to the hotel. I had rented out a whole suite for us. It had three bedrooms, a full kitchen, and a family area. After getting the bags in and everyone situated, the boys wanted to go swimming, so we just decided to go swimming together. That was a way for us to spend time together.

"Daddy, can I jump in?" Jr asked, as he stood on the edge of the pool. I told him to go head since it was only us.

"Mommy, pick me up!" Mahki yelled, as he jumped on Mimi. I looked at them and laughed. They seemed happy, and that's all that mattered to me.

"Bae, why you just staring at us like that? Have fun in the water with us." Mimi said, as she splashed water on me. I pushed her under the water like I was trying to drown her. When I let her up, she wanted to play. I tried to move past her, but she grabbed my leg, and I slipped under the water and she sat on my back. Thank God a nigga knew how to swim, cuz if not, I would be one dead nigga.

"You wanna play, Mimi?" I lifted her up then dunked her in the pool head first.

"Okay. I quit!" She laughed when she came from under the water. We continued to play until the boys announced that they were hungry, then we headed back into the hotel. I got in the shower with Mimi while the kids' nanny got them bathed and cleaned up.

Looking at Miyonna made me realize just how much I loved her. We got on each other's nerves, but at the end of the day, it was established that, neither one of us were going anywhere. I knew I was making the right choice by wanting to be with her forever. After we got out the shower, we sat down to eat.

*****

Waking up the next morning, I headed out to go and handle some business. I had decided to plan a small wedding ceremony for Miyonna and I. The most important people were there, which was just our kids. If she wanted to have a big wedding when we got home, then we could do that. I went to meet the guy by the area of the beach where I wanted the wedding to take place at. After explaining how I wanted everything set up, I headed to go and find something to wear. I texted Janetta, the kids' nanny, and told her to take Mimi out shopping for a little dress for her to wear and something for the kids to, too.

When I was done, I headed back to the hotel, and I was glad that no one was there when I got there. I hung my stuff up before going to hide the rings. I decided to lay down and take a nap while they were out and about shopping. By tomorrow night, I was going to be a married man.

When I woke up, they all were back. I washed my face and brushed my teeth before going to join them. I sat down on the couch next to Mimi. Pulling her close to me, I leaned down and kissed her on the lips quickly.

"How was y'all day?" I asked them, as I looked around.

"It was very fun." Mimi answered. "How was your day?"

"It was eventful." I chuckled.

"I can tell. Ya ass was knocked the hell out when we walked in here. I didn't want to bother you, so we stayed in here."

"Yeah. I did a lot. You'll see soon. Anyway, boys, y'all had fun?"

"Yes. I wish you were there, too." Jr said, as he came and sat next to me. I dapped him up.

"I had to handle something, but we going to have a men's night tonight. Just me, you, and your brother. Cool?"

"Yes. I'm down Pops." He said, and I smirked at my mini-me. He was already a young king. He was destined for greatness the rest of his life. I mean, his name is Juelz Johnson.

"Alright. Hold up. I'll be right back. I have to grab something really quick." I got up and walked back into the room to grab some papers. I was going to secretly get Mimi to sign the marriage license. I walked back with the marriage license and some extra pieces of notebook paper for the kids' nanny to sign to make it look legit.

"What's that?" Mimi asked.

"Uhm, insurance papers for us to get on the yacht tomorrow. Everyone over eighteen has to sign. Just in case something happens." I lied.

"Oh, okay." She said, as I was signing the papers. I walked near her so she could sign. I made sure to cover the top part so she couldn't see what it said. "I want to read it."

"I already did and took a picture of it and sent it to my lawyer earlier. It's legit. We good."

"Oh, okay. Cool." She said, before she signed the paper. I walked over to the kids' nanny and flipped the paperwork closed before putting the notebook paper on top and handing it to her for her to sign. I winked at her, and she winked back.

"You and Janetta are going to have a girls' night tonight while I'm with the boys." I told Mimi when I came back out the room and sat back down next to her.

"That's what's up. I'm with it."

"You didn't exactly have a choice in the matter. Wasn't up for debate."

"Just straight ignorant." She rolled her eyes.

"But you knew that already, and you like it. I remember when you used to stalk a nigga! I saw you outside my window a few nights." I said, seriously. She really was. I had got up to go piss in the middle of the night, and I looked out the window and saw her car parked on the opposite side of the street.

"I ain't stalk your ass. I just made sure you weren't on no slick shit. Look who your best friend is. I was ready to beat a bitch's ass quick, but you were good." Mimi said, which made me snap out of my thoughts. I had to laugh at her ass.

"Oh, that's what you calling it?" I looked at her.

"Shut your ass up!" She said, before she fell out laughing. We ended up ordering dinner, so we sat and ate as one big family. I just sat back and watched my small family. They meant the world to me outside of my mother and little brother. A nigga could be a hustla out in the streets, running the streets hard as hell, but he would be lying if he said that shit don't get old and family shit don't mean too much to them. I go hard when I'm in the streets, but being with my family is a whole other element.

Waking up the next the morning with both of my sons with me was the best feeling a nigga could have. I woke them up so that we could get shaped up, and I could get my dreads re-twisted. They weren't really that bad, cuz I had recently got them done, but I had to have everything perfect for the special day. While the boys and I were brushing our teeth, someone knocked on the door. I opened it and smiled. It was my nigga Mont and Princess. I had invited Ameerah, too, even though she not talking to me. I figured that she didn't want to miss this day. I found it funny that she wasn't talking to me, but she used my damn house to drop Princess off so that Mont can pick her up. I ain't have a problem with it, though. She my goddaughter and niece. Plus, I loved lil mama like she was my own, so I didn't mind.

"What's good man?" I shook up with him like I always did.

"Ain't shit. You ready for today?" He said as he took a seat.

"Yeah, man. Let me finish with my hygiene and shit, then I'll be back out here. If the barber and the hair stylist I hired for Princess come, let them in."

"I got you."

"Preciate it, bruh."

I walked back into the bathroom and brushed my teeth again before washing my face. I wasn't going to shower until after I got shaped up and shit. I wasn't a dirty ass nigga, so it didn't matter. I walked back to the living room with my nigga, with my sons in tow. As soon as they saw Princess, it was a wrap. They ran to her and damn near knocked her down. I guess they missed her.

"You saw, Ameerah?" He asked.

"Nah. I texted her the info and flight info. She should be here, but you know that she not really talking to no one but Mimi, so nine times out of ten, she done got her own room being that it's a surprise that y'all was coming."

"Word." Was all he said. I could tell my boy was hurting and was trying to put it on the back burner for the day.

"You good? You can talk to me, nigga. We been friends since the sandbox, nigga."

"I'm good. We can talk later. Today is your day. We about to be lit tonight." He said with a forced smile. I just shook my head. He was hard as hell to get something out of.

"Alright." I said no more about it. He would talk when he was ready.

Finally, the barber and hair stylist showed up. There were two barbers, thank God. They took care of the kids first before they got to Mont and I. An hour later, we were done and were just waiting for the girl to finish Princess' hair. I had brought her a little tiara. Everything was going to be perfect for Miyonna.

It was finally wedding time, and we were leaving out of the hotel. I looked at my youngins' and smiled. They both were handsome in their short-sleeve, button-ups and white shorts. They had some fresh white vans on their feet. I looked over at my niece, and she was looking pretty with her little white summer dress and white flats with diamonds on them. Then, she had her hair done in a bun with her small tiara on top of her head.

"You sure you ready?" Mont asked again when we made it to the beach. I nodded my head that I was. I knew that the girls should already be there and inside the tent that I had set up for them. Janetta was supposed to have her there at a certain time. I sent Princess to the tent to see if they were in there. When she pulled her little head back out and nodded that they were, then I was cool.

Mont, the boys, and I sat on the bench and waited for the officiant to get to where we were. When he finally got to the area, it was time to start. I sent a text to Janetta telling her that it was time to start. I sent the boys to the tent after making sure they had the rings in their pockets. Walking over to the officiant, I stood to the left of him with Mont to the left of me. I didn't know if we were standing right or not, but shit, he my nigga, so he was going to be standing somewhere near me.

On cue, music started, which was one of Mimi's favorite song... "1+1" by Beyoncé. I watched as Princess walked down the aisle and threw her flowers out. Then, the boys walked out behind her. Then, Ameerah and Janetta walked Mimi out with a blindfold on her face. They walked her all the way down the aisle and stopped her in front of me. She was looking pretty as hell with a fitted white dress that hugged her curves and heels that lifted her ass and had it sitting up. Her hair was up in a bun showing off her beautiful face. I was one lucky ass nigga. I walked over to her and took the blindfold off her face. She blinked a few times then looked around at everyone.

"Wh-what's going on, baby?" She asked, as she looked around at everyone.

"It's your wedding day." I smiled at her.

"Oh my god! Are you serious? This is for real?" She had a giggle in her voice.

"Yes, this is for real. You ready?"

"Yes! Yes! Yes!" She hugged me tight as hell.

"Come on! Let's do this." I grabbed her hand, and we walked up closer to the alter.

"Dearly beloved, we are gathered here today…" The officiant started the ceremony.

*****

For the reception, we had a DJ and hung out on the beach. Mimi was smiling hard as hell, and I could tell that she was happy, which was all I wanted her to be. I sat down and she sat on my lap grinding as if she was giving me a lap dance. She was making my dick hard as hell, and I was ready to give her some jail dick. You know, when inmates gotta be low when fucking, so their girl visits them with a dress or skirt on and they unzip their zipper and have their girl slide down on it. Then, slow grind on it. That's what I was ready for Mimi's ass to do at that moment.

"Let's go to the tent real quick." I told her.

"Nah. I don't want to leave the kids out here like that."

"First off, Janetta, Mont, and Ameerah out here. Second of all, you not supposed to deny your husband at all. The bible says be fruitful." I laughed.

"You are not going to be using that against me after this time." She smiled then stood up. She grabbed my hand and pulled me towards the tent. When I walked in, she closed it behind us. She kissed me, and I was ready for a quickie.

After all the festivities had wound down, we all headed back to the hotel. I ended up upgrading mine and Mimi's room to the honeymoon suite. I even paid them to decorate the room the way that I wanted it so that Mimi could be surprised when she walked in. She walked in ahead of me and hit the lights. Then, she paused and her jaw dropped. I walked around her and pulled her from the door. She fully walked into the room and had tears in her eyes. I was going to give her a tour as we christened each part of the suite.

I pulled her to the bed and kissed her, as she wrapped her arms around my neck and deepened the kiss. I reached behind her and unzipped her dress. Then, I helped her take her arms out before I let it drop down to the floor. She was standing in her strapless bra and panties. I stepped back and just stared at her body. It was perfect to me, and she was thick as hell. Her skin was so smooth.

I helped her out of her bra and panties before taking my own shirt off. I walked her over to the bed and laid her down on top of the rose petals that were laid there. I kissed her foot and worked my way up. When I got to her pussy, I watched as the wetness seeped out. I couldn't help but go in head first.

"Fuuuuuuuck!" She screamed out while palming my head. My fingers slid in and out of her as I latched onto her clit. Applying pressure, I sucked it into my mouth like I was milking it. Before I knew it, she was cumming, but I wasn't done with her, though. I leaned up to her lips and kissed her while I rubbed on her pussy. It was getting wetter and wetter, so I headed back down. I kissed her stomach trailing the kisses down. When I got back to her pussy, I spread her lips open and used the tip of my tongue to tickle her clit making her giggle.

"Stop playing, bae." She told me.

"Your shit wet as hell." I let her know.

"Stop teasing me. Just stick it in already."

"Patience."

"Fuck all that!" She said as she sat up. She scooted back before crawling to me. She started to unbutton my pants. I tried to stop her, but she smacked my hands away. I couldn't help but laugh, as she yanked my pants down, along with my boxers. I took over from there after that.

Andrea

I sat on the bed next to her and was about to pull her on top of me when she took me deep into her mouth. I bit my lip to avoid yelling out like a little bitch. I grabbed her head as it bobbed up and down. She was going hard as fuck on my dick. She started playing with my balls in her right hand while still sucking. I was getting too close to letting go.

"Shiiiit! Suck that shit, Mimi!" I groaned, and she started sucking faster. I was cumming, but she wouldn't stop, though. "Shit! Fucking bitch!" I got a tight grip on her hair and yanked her head back. She looked at me and licked her lips. She didn't even care that she could have had a bald spot. She reached down and grabbed my dick stroking it. She was bringing him back to life. When he was hard enough, I pulled her on my lap, then slammed her down on him. She wrapped her legs around me and her arms around my neck before she started to move up and down on me slowly. I grabbed her ass cheeks and squeezed them, as I felt her getting wetter. I smacked her on the ass, and that made her speed up. She started bouncing on my dick like she was on one of them bouncy balls with handles. I grabbed onto her waist.

"Slow down some." I told her.

"Nah. You wanted to me speed up." She replied, as she stopped and got into a squatting position. Holding onto my shoulder. She really started to ride my dick, then, and I couldn't do shit but go along for the ride.

"Shhhhhhh! I'm 'bout to cum! "Fucker!" She yelled out.

"Cum then!" I told her, as I pulled her all the way back down. I could tell that she was cumming, because she tried to sit still. I flipped us over before pulling out of her and rolling her on her stomach. I arched her back bringing her ass in the air before sliding back inside of her. I held onto her waist and gave her slow, deep strokes until she clapped her ass cheeks enticing me. I grabbed a tight hold of her hair pulling it out of the bun that it was in. I sped up smacking my pelvic area into her.

"Fuuuuuuuck!" She yelled out.

"Throw that ass back girl!" I smacked her on the ass a few times.

"Shhhhhhh! Oh my god!" She cried.

"Throw all that ass on your husband, girl!" I popped her on the ass a few times.

"I-I'm 'bout to cum." She said, then I felt her juices run down my dick. I kept going, then I was cumming. Afterward, I laid on top of her back trying to catch my breath.

"Damn. I love you, husband."

"I love you, too, wife." I kissed her. We fucked and made love the rest of the night well into the morning. I was ready for life with my wife.

. . .

The wedding and honeymoon were all over, and we were back home. We had officially been married for three weeks now. We were going together to tell our parents. I didn't see why she wanted to tell her bitch ass mother, but if she really wanted to, then that's whatever.

We were heading over to my mother's house first. I made sure to text my little brother so that he could be there, too. When I pulled up, both of their cars were there. We even brought the kids with us to smooth things over with my mom when she gets mad about not being invited to the wedding. We walked up to the door, and I used my key to get inside. I heard the television, so I followed the sound to the living room.

"Hey, Ma." I said.

"G-Ma!" The boys ran to her.

"Hello, my babies. How are y'all?" She asked.

"We good." They ran and sat on the couch. She turned and looked at us. Mimi smiled at her.

"Don't be standing there with that cheesy ass smile. Y'all asses up to something. How many months are you?" She looked at Mimi's stomach making mine and my brother's eyes follow hers.

"I'm not pregnant. That's not why we wanted to talk." She brushed my mom off.

"So what y'all want to talk about?" She asked.

"Uh, we're married!" Mimi told her and damn near shoved her hand in my mom's face. I fell out laughing, cuz it looked like my mom was going to smack her at first.

"I ought to whoop your tall ass. Why were we not invited?" She snapped. My brother and Mimi both chuckled.

"To my defense, I didn't know about this until I was standing at the altar. They took the blindfold off my eyes, and Juelz was standing in front of me with some dude behind him." Mimi threw me under the bus.

"I apologize, Ma. I wanted it to be a surprise." I told her.

"Maybe one day we will have a wedding where everyone is invited and you will be the first one to know and be invited."

"Don't try and butter me up!"

"I'm not."

"Okay."

"Congrats, bro and sis." My brother dapped me then hugged Mimi. "I hope I gain a niece out of this marriage now." He smiled at us. I simply looked at Mimi.

"I hope so, too. I got baby fever bad, and I really don't want another boy, so I'm going to pray forever until it happens."

"I'm going to pray with you." My mom chimed in. We stayed with my mom for a little while before we headed to Mimi's mom house.

When we pulled up, Mimi took a deep breath before she got out the car. I grabbed the boys, and we walked behind her. She walked up and knocked on the door. Her little sister opened the door.

"Hey, Ju." She spoke to me.

"Sup."

"Hi, Miyonna. Come in." She smiled. I thought she was going to say something smart, but I guess not.

Andrea

"What you doing here, Miyonna?" Her mother asked.

"Mom, we came over here to tell you that we were married."

"That's a damn shame. I wonder who proposed to who." She said, smartly.

"Excuse me!" Miyonna snapped at her.

"You think you're a man. Look at what you do, so like I said, I wonder who proposed to who."

"You know damn well Juelz proposed to me years ago. Then, he surprised me with the wedding."

"Hmm."

"Hmm, what? You always have an opinion. Why can't you just say congratulations and be done with the bullshit?" Miyonna snapped at her.

"Fine, I'll say something then be done with it. I think Juelz is less of a man to let you do what you do and not have an opinion about it. It's clear who wears the pants and who wears the dresses and skirts. Now I am done." She got quiet, then said something again. "He must feel like you a man, because he didn't even call me to have me walk you down the aisle since your father isn't here. That says a lot, so have a nice day young men." She said, and Miyonna's sister laughed.

I grabbed both of my sons' hands with one of my hands and pulled Mimi with the other one, and we headed for the door. Mimi was hyped as hell like she wanted to fight. I looked back and saw that her mother had a smirk on her face.

When we got to the car, I let her go and helped the boys in the car.

"I'm happy for y'all," Miyonna's brother said when he ran out to us.

"Thank you." Mimi said before hugging him. "I'll call you later. I'm not about to play with your mother and sister."

"Yeah. Lil sis bugging. Can I come over your house?"

"Sure."

"Thanks. I'll follow y'all in my car." Owen said, before walking to his car. After I got in the car, we pulled off. Today was one eventful day.

Chapter 10: Miyonna Pierce- Johnson

Today was one long ass day. I was glad that our parents knew even though my mom and sister pissed me the fuck off. I was ready to just go home and relax. I knew that I couldn't really do that, because Ameerah called on our way home saying that she wanted to talk to me about something. I already knew that it was about whatever was going on with her and Mont. I found it funny that she wasn't talking to Juelz, but she was talking to me kind of and she used our house to do drop offs. I was surprised when they showed up for the wedding and actually got along. They partied like they weren't beefing. I was glad that they enjoyed themselves, at least long enough for that. I was glad that my brother came over, too. I missed him, because he worked a lot so that when he turns eighteen, he can move out. I was proud that he had a legit job while going to school.

When we got into the house, I started to cook dinner while I waited for Ameerah to show up. I pulled out some wine and two glasses and sat them on the counter. I knew she was probably going to need it. I continued to move around the kitchen until I heard Juelz say that Ameerah was here, then she walked in, and I could see the stress on her face.

"What's going on? You okay?" I asked her as she sat down on the stool.

"I'm hurt, confused, mad as hell, everything. Like Mont has a baby mama that's not me. Then, he expects for everything to be okay." She said, and my eyes got big as hell.

"He got a what? Who is she? Did you see her?" I rambled off question and question.

"Yeah. I saw her. She was at the hospital sitting in his room when I walked in there that time when I stabbed him."

"Bitch, that was weeks ago. Why you just now saying something?"

"I was hurt. I feel like your man knew and didn't throw me a hint or anything. It was like everything was cool. I didn't really trust anyone. Then, I thought about it and realized that he didn't really have to tell me anything, because Mont is his friend. I was mad at you at first, too. I thought you knew. Then, I thought about that, too, and I realized that Juelz wouldn't tell you anything if he knew because he knows that you would just tell me."

"Right! So what happened at the hospital?"

"I put the girl out and acted like everything was all good. You know I act like the perfect girl in public. When no one was in the room, I plucked his IV tube hard."

"Petty."

"So what! He should consider himself lucky to still be alive, but that's not even the kicker."

"Girl, what?" I asked. I was too nosey right now.

"It was one of his old bitches that he cheated with before. Like, her pussy must have been bomb as fuck if he dipped back with the bitch."

"Okay. I have one question, and don't be mad at me for asking."

"Okay. What is it?"

"Are you sure she is his baby's mother? Like, she could have told you that to get under your skin. Do you see a child or did she look pregnant?"

"She didn't tell me, Mimi. He did." She said, and my mouth dropped open.

"Ooh! Girl, yeah it's true. You know Mont not going to lie." She was about to say something, but Juelz walked in with Mont behind him, and Ameerah got quiet as hell.

"What y'all in here talking about?" Juelz asked, and I simply shrugged my shoulders.

"Girl talk." Ameerah answered before chuckling. I didn't say anything. I guess the silence got too awkward for them, because they walked out then I heard the door to the basement open then close.

"Nosey ass niggas!" I spat.

"For real." She agreed.

"Anyways. Where Princess at?"

"With my mom. You know they spoil her." She had the nerve to say.

"Everybody spoil her."

"True." We laughed.

"So, I want you to get your mind off everything you have going on. I think that we should have a girls' night this Friday." I threw it out there.

"Bitch, what other friends you got beside me?" She asked with a side-eye.

"I got a few. Don't worry about it."

"Hmm." She sipped her wine.

"Hush. So, you down or not?"

"Yeah. I'm game, but right now, I am about to go before Mont comes back upstairs. Not in the mood for all that today." She stood up and looked behind her.

"You have to talk to him one day. You still love him, and he's the father of your child."

"You are so right, but that won't be today. See you later." She hugged me. "Love you."

"Love you, too." I said, as I shook my head. She walked out the kitchen, and a few minutes later, I heard the door close behind her. I pulled my phone out and texted Drea to see what she was doing.

Me: You busy?"

Drea: Not really. Just picked my son up and literally just walked in the house.

Me: I'm coming over in like a half hour

Drea: okay. That's cool.

Me: make sure the girls are all there

Drea: got you

Andrea

I sat my phone to the side and finished cooking. When it was done, I made everyone's plate before calling them down to come and eat.

"Bae, I'll be right back. I need to go do something really quick." I told Juelz when he sat down.

"Alright. Be careful."

"I will." I kissed him before turning to my little brother. "Owen, don't stay here too late. You do have school tomorrow, and I don't want to hear Mommy's mouth more than what I already do. Okay?"

"Alright. I was going to leave after I ate, anyway." He smirked.

"Word. Love you."

"Love you, too." I hugged him, then grabbed my phone and headed for the door. I made it to Drea's house after twenty minutes and was glad that everyone was there. That way, I could say what I had to say then head back home.

Ringing the door, I was glad when someone came and opened it; it felt like I was outside for a while.

"Dang, took y'all long enough to open up." I said, as I walked through.

"Nobody wanted to get up for real." Rome said. I just looked at her. She was one of the chicks on Drea's team. She was cool, but she just always had something smart to say. But hey, that was her.

"A damn shame. Anyway, I wanted to talk to y'all about something."

118

"What's up?"

"So my best friend is going through some things, and I wanted to have a girls' night. You know, alcohol, laughter, all that. I want all y'all to be there. We ain't got no friends, just us, and I'm cool with y'all, so I figured that we all can just hang out. Let our hair down and be chill."

"Okay. You could have told me that through text, and I would have passed it on." Drea said with a confused look on her face.

"No I couldn't, because I need a favor, and I needed all of y'alls undivided attention when I say what I have to say."

"Okay. What's up?"

"When we all chilling, I need y'all to keep it on the hush about what I do. Don't mention Pocha. Don't mention any of that. She doesn't know nothing about my savage lifestyle, so shut the fuck up and act like we all just friends that happen to know each other. We met one day and the rest is history. Feel me?"

"I got you." Drea said.

"We got you, too." They all chimed in.

"Thank you. I will text y'all the address and stuff. Everyone bring a bottle. The more alcohol, the better. I will cover food and stuff." I let them know as I looked at my phone.

"Word. I'm bringing my rum and pineapple cupcakes."

"No comment. See y'all this Friday." I headed towards the door, but when I got in my car, I suddenly got the strange feeling that someone was following me. I discreetly looked around but nothing seemed out the norm. I knew someone was following me, because that feeling never stirred me wrong.

I hurried and text Dun to let him know what was up before I made a detour. I wasn't about to drive straight home with someone tailing me. I had to think about my kids. I ended up having Dun meet me at one of our safe houses. When I got there, I realized that no one was around, so I guess that I had lost whoever it was.

"You good?" Dun asked when we walked over to me.

"Man, I guess so. You know my sixth sense never stirs me wrong. I had a strong feeling that someone was behind me. When I made the detour, I lost them. Just follow me home."

"Alright. I got you. I'mma be like two cars behind you."

"Thank you!"

"You don't have to thank me. You my nigga for a reason." He said with a chuckle.

"Shut up. Let's go." I got in my car and pulled off. I was glad when I got home. After waiving at Dun, I used my key and walked inside. I walked in the kitchen and was surprised that it was clean and the food was put away. I went upstairs and checked on the boys before walking into my bedroom. Juelz was sitting at the foot of the bed playing the game. He paused it when he saw me.

"Why you look like that? What happened?" He sat the controller down.

"Someone was following me, so I had to detour, which is why I am just now getting home."

"What? Why didn't you call me?"

"I figured that you were here by yourself with the boys. Why would you bring them out like that? So, I called Dun." I tried to mumble the last part.

"The fuck!" He yelled, making me jump. "I'm your fucking man. Your fucking husband. This ain't have shit to do with street shit, so I'm confused as to why you would call him before your own nigga. Either, this street really getting to your head, or you fucking or have fucked that nigga, so which is it?" He walked closer to me.

"Neither. Why would you even say some shit like that?"

"Fuck all that shit! You on that shit, but it's all good. I'mma say a word to Dun ass. Go ahead and do what the fuck it was that you were about to do." He was mad. I looked at him, as he grabbed his weed and rolled up. My baby was fine. He had his dreads braided in two braids. Shape-up was all fresh and what not. I wanted to walk over and sit on his dick, but being that he was mad, he would probably push me off. I turned and walked into the bathroom to go and take a shower.

After I was done with my shower, I threw on a lace bra and panty set before putting lotion on and crawling into the bed. I got under the covers quietly and grabbed my kindle so that I could try and read something. That wasn't really working, because I kept staring at Juelz. I knew that he felt my eyes burning the back of his head. I couldn't take it anymore. I got from under the cover and crawled over to him. I kissed the back of his neck before throwing my arms around him and kissing his face. My feelings were hurt when he pushed me off him.

"Go hug and kiss on Dun!" He said, when he turned and looked at me. My mouth dropped open, and he looked satisfied before he turned his head back and focused on the game. I just went back and crawled under the cover. I threw the blanket over my head so he couldn't see the tears in my eyes. I felt extra emotional and not wanted. I just closed my eyes and forced myself to sleep.

. . .

It was finally Friday, and I was so glad for this girls' day. The Johnson household was quiet as hell being that Juelz still wasn't talking to me. He was acting like a bitch ass nigga, and I really didn't like it. Did I bring it on myself? I didn't think so, but of course, Juelz thought that I did. I wasn't about to argue with him, though. I kissed both of the boys and told them that I would see them later.

"They spending the night at my mom's tonight. She misses them."

"Could have asked my opinion but whatever." I said to him with the roll of eyes.

"Who the fuck is you talking to? I'm not that nigga that's about to bow down to you. You got me fucked up. Go ahead with yourself before you have hurt feelings. Bye yo!"

122

"Whatever!" I walked out the door and slammed it behind me. I sat the stuff in the backseat before getting in the front and pulling off. Juelz and his attitude were on my mind as I rode to pick up Ameerah then went to meet up with the girls. When I pulled up to her mom's house, I pushed him to the back of my mind. Well, I tried to.

"Hey, Mimi." Ameerah said, as she got in the car.

"What's up? You ready for the night?" I asked her as we pulled off.

"Yeah. I need this. I have been working all week long. I sold a house and the guy has been hell."

"Oh, damn." Was all I said.

"Oh, Lord, what's wrong?" She looked at me.

"Nothing. I just want to enjoy my night with the girls. It's just shit with Juelz." I brushed it off.

"Oh. Men problems. That's what tonight is for. We going to drink it off." She said with a smile.

"Yes, we are." I smiled back.

I planned to get drunk as hell, then go home, and be really nasty with Juelz. Sucking dick till I threw up. That would make him not be mad at me anymore. I was glad when we pulled up to the spot. I had Ameerah help me carry the things from the backseat inside.

"Hey, girls!" I said, as I walked inside. I hugged them all and introduced everyone as I sat the food down on the table.

"I'm ready to eat and drink, then talk shit about niggas." Drea said with a chuckle.

"Me, too." I added, as I fixed me a small plate and a drink. I had to have something strong.

"Let's make a toast." Ameerah lifted her glass. Everyone else followed. "Let's make a toast to these fuck niggas and not letting them fuck with us."

"I think a fuck nigga been fucking with you which is why we are here." Drea said to Ameerah, and we all fell out laughing.

"Forget y'all! Anyways…" She rolled her eyes.

"Let's just drink. Dance. Chill, too." I said.

"That's a bet. Even though I'm not really a dancer. I'll just sip my drink." Rome, one of Drea's girls chimed in.

"Word." I nodded.

We all sat around drinking and laughing just enjoying our time until my phone started vibrating off the hook. I grabbed the phone and looked at it. Of course it was Juelz calling me. I ignored the call, then looked at the time and saw that it was way after midnight. I didn't care, though. It was Friday night, and my kids weren't home. Plus, I was chilling with my girls. After setting my phone down, I grabbed my cup and poured another drink.

"Let's take shots!" Drea yelled out. Shit, I was down. She pulled the glasses out and started to pour shots. Everyone took one. "Fuck all fuck niggas and their side bitches, too!" She yelled out before we all took the shot.

"Whew!" I yelled out. That shit burned my chest. I patted it, but I wanted to take another one. "Let's take another one!"

We continued to take shots until the bottle was gone, and we started on the next one. I was having so much fun. I grabbed my phone and looked at it. I laughed when I saw that I had almost twenty missed calls and a bunch of text messages, all from Juelz. I didn't care; that's why I turned my ringer off and had it on silent.

"Mimi, Juelz is calling my phone like crazy."

"Oh, well! Fuck him. Ignore him." I told her before drinking the rest of my cup.

"Okay. Well, fuck him then!" She laughed, making everyone else laugh.

"Y'all ever think about having more kids?" Someone asked, and I was so drunk that I didn't even know who it was.

"Nope! My daughter is a handful." I heard Ameerah say, because she was sitting right next to him.

"You, Mimi?"

"I want a daughter then I will be complete." I slurred.

"Cheers to Mimi going home and getting all the dick that she can tonight!" Ameerah lifted her glass.

"CHEERS!" everyone called out. We hung out a little while longer before I announced that I was going home.

"None of us can drive. Let's call Shore or Uber."

"I'll call Shore. I think that's safer." I offered. After fumbling with my phone, I was finally able to get the cab company on the phone. After calling the cab, we attempted to clean up. I don't think that worked, though. We walked to the door when we heard a car pull up.

Andrea

As soon as we opened the door and walked out, gunshots rang out. I saw that the cab driver was slumped over. I was reaching for my own gun when I felt a bullet pierce my arm. That didn't stop me, though. I felt something skid across my head then my back. When I felt more bullets start to riddle my body, I was already going down. I could hear gunshots and people yelling as everything started to fade to black.

Chapter 11: Ameerah Statum

I couldn't believe that someone shot Mimi. When the gunshots stopped, I ran over to her. I was drunk as hell, but that shit sobered me quick. She fell out in my arms, and I was screaming for someone to call 911. I wasn't sure if they called or not. I was talking to Mimi to make sure she could hear me. The girls were checking to make sure everything was okay.

"Mimi! Can you hear me? Miyonna! Open your eyes!" I cried.

"Check her pulse!" I heard someone yell out to me. I checked, but I didn't feel anything, and that made me start to really panic.

"I don't feel nothing. There is no pulse. Where the fuck is the ambulance?"

"I hear the sirens. They coming now."

The ambulance pulled up, and they damn near pushed me out the way to get to Mimi, but I didn't even care. As long as they took care of her, and she wasn't dead. I made sure to take all her stuff. I looked in her purse and grabbed her keys, and I was surprised when I saw that she had a gun in there.

"I'm going to drive her car and follow the ambulance. I will meet y'all there." I dug in my purse, grabbed two mints, and popped them into my mouth. When they finally loaded her up, I got in her car and pulled off behind them. I knew that I had to call Juelz, but that was some yelling that I wasn't really trying to hear at the moment. I decided to wait until I got to the hospital. We all pulled up at the same time, and I parked near the door and jumped out. I ran behind them as they rolled Mimi to the back.

"Excuse ma'am. You cannot go back there. Please sit down in the waiting room." The paramedic said, as they wheeled her back and let the door shut behind them. I walked to the corner and sat down.

Pulling out Mimi's phone, I released a breath and called Juelz.

"Miyonna! Where the fuck you at?" He yelled when he answered.

"Juelz, this isn't Mimi. It's me, Meerah. Come to Monmouth Medical Center. Mimi was shot.

"The fuck! I know you didn't just say that my wife was shot. Maaaan! I'm on my way right now." He said, then hung the phone up. I dropped her phone in my purse and leaned back in my chair. I closed my eyes wishing that this was all a nightmare that I was living. My eyes flew open when hurricane Juelz came through the door yelling. I looked and saw that he had Mont with him. He walked over to the receptionist's desk and punched on the window a few times. I think the lady was scared.

"Bitch, I don't know why you trying to call security when you need to be trying to call a hairstylist to cover up that alopecia in that wig. Anyway, what the fuck is going on with my fucking wife, Miyonna Pierce-Johnson?"

"Sh-she is in surgery, sir. I don't know anything yet. The doctor will be out soon. Please have a seat."

"Bitch, go sit in a hairdresser's chair somewhere!" I chuckled, before I walked over to him and touched his back. He turned around like he was ready to swing so I backed up some.

"Calm down, Ju. She in surgery." I told him. He looked at me and pulled me in for a hug before letting me.

"Damn. All that is her blood?" He asked, and I nodded. "What the fuck happened?"

"I don't know. All I know is that we were walking out to catch a cab, and as soon as we went outside, shots rang out like crazy. It sounded like it was hella people shooting. The cab driver got shot first. Then, it was like whoever it was that was shooting was gunning right for Mimi, because she was the only one to get shot. The other girls that we were with shot back and hit someone, but the other two got away. I don't know what happened after that, because I got on the ground to check Mimi and wait for the ambulance." I explained to him. By now, I was in tears.

"Fuck! I tried to catch this shit before it happened." Juelz snapped before walking away from me.

"What you mean? You know who the fuck did this?" I snapped, and Mont grabbed me pulling me into a tight bear hug.

"Calm down, bae. It's not the time." Mont had the nerve to say.

"Fuck you! Y'all keeping secrets and shit." I snapped with tears still running. "Y'all ain't shit. I hope you know that Mimi didn't have a pulse at all. I don't think they found one either unless they did when she was in the ambulance, but since y'all got secrets, I guess y'all don't care." I said to Mont and Juelz before kicking my foot backward hitting Mont in his dick to get him off me. I walked back to the corner and sat back down. I didn't want to talk to anyone until the doctor came.

Time passed and passed. Miyonna's mom, sister, and brother all came to the hospital. Tiyonna was crying, and Owen looked mad as hell, but neither one of them were saying anything at all. Miyonna's mom had a weird expression on her face. She didn't look sad or emotional. I guess people dealt with things differently. I shrugged her off and closed my eyes, attempting to take a nap while I waited for the doctor to come out.

The sun was up and everything, and we still hadn't heard anything. I knew that the shift was about to switch. This could only mean that something was wrong if it's taking this long for them to come out and tell us something.

About an hour later, the doctor walked out looking for Juelz. We all stood up behind him. He introduced himself, but no one really wanted to hear that. I guess he could tell that by the way that we were grilling him.

"Okay. Mrs. Johnson was shot in the arm, chest, stomach, back, and a bullet grazed her forehead. She flat-lined a few times, but we managed to save her. The bullet that hit her stomach just missed the baby by a half of inch. We are monitoring the baby as much as we can…"

"BABY!" We all said.

"Yes. She appears to be about ten weeks pregnant. We have her in a medically-induced coma, because her body needs to heal. No one can go in and see her. We want to wait a full twenty-four hours before allowing any visitors."

"Okay. Thank you, Doctor." Juelz told him.

"You're welcome. I will be here for the next twenty-four hours to make sure everything is okay and going well." The doctor said before turning to head back to the back. I decided to just go home to shower and check on Princess.

"Oh my gosh! Where did all that blood come from?" My mom asked when I walked in. She had Princess sitting next to her on the couch.

"Come to my room with me. Princess, finish watching the movie."

"Okay, Mommy." We walked to the back, and I started to take my clothes off as I explained everything that happened to my mom. When I was done, I had tears in my eyes again, and she was crying, too. It was a lot to deal with.

"Ameerah, th-there is something that I want to tell you. It's kind of important." My mom started to say. I looked at her.

Andrea

"What is it?" I asked her. She started to say something, but it was like nothing was coming out. I squinted my eyes and looked at her. "Ma, what's up?"

"I don't know how to say this." She said before breaking down. I pulled her in and hugged her tightly. My mom and I never really had that extra tight relationship. I loved her, but we weren't the best of friends.

"It's okay, Mom. It will come out when it's supposed to come out." I had told her before I stood up to go and get in the shower.

When I got out the shower, I couldn't sleep, so I decided to just take Princess out and spend the day with her since she would be the perfect thing to get my mind off of everything. After getting us both dressed, we headed out and ended up at the nail salon, then we went to iPlay America for a few hours. Our last spot was Toys "R" Us.

As we were going up and down the aisles, my phone rang. I knew it was Mont, because I knew his number by heart, even though his number wasn't saved.

"Hello?"

"Where you at?" He asked.

"In Toys "R" Us with the princess. She tearing the store up." I chuckled.

"Word. I'm about to pull up. Don't leave. For real! I'mma be there in like ten minutes. Matter of fact, stay on the phone with me until I get there." He said ,and I fell out laughing.

"Mommy, who that?" Princess' nosey ass asked. I just shook my head. She too much.

"It's Daddy."

"Ooooh. Can I talk to him? Please, Mommy." She begged.

"No. I'm talking to him."

"Stop being jealous. Put my baby on the phone, yo." He laughed. I passed the phone to her and watched as she talked to her dad. She was too much. I felt like my baby was four going on twenty-one. She handed me the phone, and I saw that he had hung up, then I heard someone call my name. I looked up and saw that it was him walking towards us. Princess ran to him full speed, as I pushed the cart and walked over to them.

"How you feeling?" He asked.

"I'm trying to be okay. Princess is kind of taking my mind off things. How is Juelz?"

"He alright. He went back to the hospital and shit. He said he was about to have a thorough talk with the doctor, so he was going to call me back."

"Oh, okay. I'm going back to the hospital tomorrow. Why is everyone so hush about shit? Is something going on that I don't know about?" I asked him, because I remember the girls whispering about something. They were calling Mimi by the name of Pocha, but I acted like I didn't hear them so that I could listen some more.

"I don't know, Meerah." He said, and I knew that he was lying.

"Whatever! Come on, Princess. Let's finish shopping." I walked around him with Princess holding onto the cart. Of course, Mont was behind us, but I didn't care. I just ignored his ass.

"You acting childish as hell right now."

"I don't care. Y'all niggas keeping secrets like my best friend's not laid the fuck up. Y'all corny as hell for that!"

"We corny because we won't tell you somebody else's business? Word?"

"Whatever!" I rolled my eyes and focused my attention back on Princess. This wasn't even in my character to be arguing in public, so I was just going to shut my ass up. I was so glad when Princess said that she was hungry, so we went and paid for the toys and everything that she picked up so that we could leave.

"I want Burger King so I could play in the playroom." She let us know. I should have known.

"Okay." Was all I said. Burger King was in the same plaza as the Toys "R" Us, so we only had to drive across the parking lot. Mont told us to sit down while he went and ordered the food.

"Mommy, are we going home with Daddy? I miss my room and my bed." Princess asked, and I looked up from my phone to look at her. Looking at her face made me feel bad as hell.

"Maybe you can go home with Daddy."

"No. I want all of us. Kerro misses you, too."

134

"I will think about it." I told her, and she smiled.

"Don't forget, Mommy. Okay?"

"Yes. I won't forget." About ten minutes later, Mont was finally coming back with the food. We sat and ate while Princess ran her mouth with Mont. Looking at them interact had me thinking that, maybe I handled things wrong when I found out about his baby mama. I didn't even attempt to hear anything that he said. I knew that I had to have the conversation with Mont, but I was scared that he was going to tell me some shit that I really didn't want to hear. At the same time, I had to be an adult about it, because obviously, all my decisions affect our daughter. I was so wrapped up in my thoughts that I didn't even realize that Princess had finished her food and was off to the playroom.

"Ameerah! You staring at a nigga like you miss him." Mont snapped me out of my trance.

"I do miss you. I won't lie about that."

"You miss me but won't bring your ass home."

"So. I still feel a type of way. We need to have a talk before any coming home even happens."

"We can talk now." I looked around then at him like he was crazy.

"No we can't. We are not having a talk like that out in the open for the world to hear."

"Come to the house tonight then. Ain't like we can go to the hospital and shit."

"Alright. I will come to the house, but I am sleeping in the guest room. I don't want you to try anything."

"Girl, you know damn well that pussy and everything else on and inside your body belongs to me."

"Oh, really? So, what if I told you that I fucked someone else since I left? Or what if I said that I let a nigga get a little taste?" I asked. Just playing with him, but he didn't need to know that I was playing.

"What if I told you that I'mma smack the shit out of you and body that nigga?" He asked with a mean mug on his face.

"Fix your face." I smiled at him.

"I'm not playing with you. Who the fuck is the nigga?" He started to get loud making me look around. People was staring at us. I politely grabbed my purse and stood up. I decided to walk away, because I hated for people to be in my business like that. I felt Mont walking behind me, but I refused to turn around and look. "I know you hear me talking to you."

"Instead of following me out the door, go get our daughter." I walked to my car and got in. When I saw him walk out with Princess, I pulled off. I decided to go to my office for a little while.

"He,y Ameerah. I didn't know that you were coming in today." My assistant said as she followed me into my office.

"I didn't know I was coming here today. You know I don't do weekends."

"Exactly. You okay?"

"Yeah. I'm cool. You know the guy that just bought a house, right?"

"Yeah. He was cute. What about him?"

"Girl, you don't even like men. Anyway, he has been texting me about the house. I keep telling him that after he buys the house, what he does is up to him. I feel like it's a ploy for me to come over there, but at the same time, you know how I am with my clients, so I want you to come with me. I don't really trust him like that."

"Damn. You know I got you, though. When we going?"

"Today. So, come on." I told her before grabbing some files and standing up.

"Oh, you got new potential clients, too. I filled in the appointment slots for you and stuff." That's why I fucked with her. She was the best assistant ever.

"Cool. I want to have a meeting with you in a few days about something, but for now, let's handle this."

"Okay." We drove to the house while talking about everything business wise. When we pulled up, I got a weird feeling over me, but I brushed it off. "You told dude to meet us here?"

"Yeah. He just now pulling up." I pointed. When dude got out the car and walked over to us, I felt his eyes burning a hole through me. "So what's going on?"

"I need to talk to you in private."

"This is my assistant. It's cool if she is present."

"I just need to talk to you in private real quick. Not going to take long." He said.

"Okay." We walked inside and stood in the foyer while my assistant went and got in the car. I saw her start making calls. "What's up?"

"You been on my mind since the first day I saw you. I wanted to ask you on a date."

"Woah. I'm not single. I would never disrespect my man like that." I let him know.

"I'm sure you been with him for years, and he still didn't put a ring on your finger, so maybe you don't mean much to dude. Haven't you heard that you are single until you get married?" He smiled, making me roll my eyes.

"I have heard that, but it doesn't apply to me. I…" I got cut off by someone banging on the door and ringing the doorbell excessively. I walked over and opened the door since I was slightly uncomfortable with the conversation. As soon as I opened it, I wanted to close it right back. It was Mont. I feel like I was caught cheating.

"What the fuck you doing here with this nigga?" He snapped. I turned, and dude was standing behind me. "So this the dude you fucked and who ate your pussy?"

"What? No. I swear I was joking when I said that. He is a client. I sold him this house. You walked past my assistant sitting right in the front seat of my car."

"Fuck all that!" He grabbed my arm. "Get your purse and let's go." Shit, he ain't have to tell me twice. I was so embarrassed. After I grabbed my purse, he damn near dragged me out the house. He walked me to my car, opened the door, and shoved me inside.

"Ouch!"

"Shut up. I'mma follow you to the house."

"I have to drop her off at the office so she can get her car."

"Alright. Let's go!" He said then walked to his car. I was too embarrassed to look at anyone. I couldn't believe Mont, and dude was talking all that shit, then bitched up when Mont popped up. Bitch ass nigga. I pulled off, and it was a quiet ride to my office, then I went to our house. It was a long day, and I needed a nap, so I can be rested enough to be at the hospital all day with Mimi tomorrow.

Chapter 12: Juelz Johnson

It had been a month, and Mimi was still in the hospital in the coma. I was surprised that the baby was still hanging on in there. It was hard as hell coming to the hospital and seeing her like that. I was talking to her, but she wasn't responding, and this was too much for me to handle. Then, on top of being at the hospital, I was taking care of the boys. They were asking for their mom all the time, and I told them about her being in the hospital, but it wasn't like they really understood what was going on. To top it off, we were looking for the fucker who shot her. My plate was full, so I had Mont handling our business.

"Yo, did you find out who it was that was laid out that night Mimi was hit up?" I asked Mont, when he walked into the hospital room.

"That was that nigga Vin that was laid out. You know who he run with, right?" He asked, and I looked.

"Who?" I asked.

"Member that old head, Luther, that Xavier had beef with?" He asked, and I nodded. "That nigga Vin and his boy Ben and them work for Luther. He been trying to get niggas to cop from him for a while so he probably figured that if he axed Mimi off and she was dead like her father, then he would have niggas copping from him."

"Nigga done fucked up!" I snapped. I was about to say something else but stopped when Ameerah walked in with her arms folded like she had an attitude, but I ignored her ass. I don't know who she thought she was fazing, cuz I surely was not fazed at all.

"What y'all talking 'bout?" Ameerah asked, and I ignored her. I went and sat back in my chair near Miyonna's bed.

"Mind your business!" Mont told her, and I chuckled.

"No. I heard y'all conversation. And…" She started, but Mont cut her off.

"And what you going to do about it? Nothing. Now, sit your ass down somewhere." Mont told her, and I fell out laughing when she sat down.

"Bae, you need to get up and see your girl. She all soft and shit." I said, looking at Mimi.

"Yeah, Mimi. It's time to get up. Your husband and his best friend are so annoying, and I can't deal with them on my own." Ameerah said to Miyonna. I saw her starting to tear up. Mont reached over and hugged her, but she pushed him back. They always beefing with each other.

"Oh, you don't want me to touch you, but your other niggas can?" Mont smirked at her. I just looked at them.

"Shut up!" she snapped at him.

"You got a side nigga, Meerah? For real?" I asked her.

"Oh my gosh! Shut the hell up! No I don't, and if I did, why would y'all even be talking about this in public like this?"

"You acting shy?" I asked her.

Andrea

"Hush."

"Alright. But if y'all are about to start arguing and shit, get out! I need a calm setting in here. Y'all niggas need to chill the fuck out." I let them know before they really started to bug the fuck out.

"We good." Mont just smirked. I just minded my business. I needed to talk to him about some business. I got his attention for him to get Ameerah to leave for a minute. He got the hint. "Aye, Meerah, can you go get me something to eat and call and check on Princess and the boys for me?"

"You just trying to get rid of me, but I'll do it. I'll be right back." She said, as she grabbed her bag and headed for the door. I was glad that Mont closed the door behind her.

"What's up?" He asked. "I can see that you thinking something."

"I wanna get all of us together. Them hit bitches, our crew, and Dun. All of us together, and we can handle this shit. Niggas have to be caught before she up." I told him.

"I feel you. We got this, though."

"Word." Was all I said before I buzzed the nurse in the room. She walked in, and I asked her to get the doctor. Mont walked out when they walked back in. I asked them for an update on Mimi and the baby.

"Her arm is healed. Her forehead was fine, because it was only a graze. The bullet to the back went straight through, but didn't hit anything major."

"What about the bullet to the stomach?"

"We carefully removed it. We are not really out the woods yet, because of the baby being in there."

"How is the baby?"

"The baby is okay. The heartbeat is stronger than what I expected it to be, but we are monitoring it closely as you can see. That's what the belt thing is across her stomach."

"Okay. Thank you."

"We lowered the dosage of meds. Waking up is up to her. It should be any day now. I guess when her body is well-rested, she will wake up. All up to her."

"Okay. Thank you, Doctor." I shook his hand before he walked out the room. I walked over to Mimi's bed and stared down at her. Then, I grabbed her hand and kissed it.

"It's time to get up for real. Shit getting thick out here. Plus, we need to go to real doctor's appointments and shit. I'm going to bring the boys here to see you. Hopefully, you can wake up and respond to them." I said to her. The door opened, and Mont walked back in with Ameerah.

"We got you some pizza. You need to eat. That's not healthy. You be sitting here all day and shit." Ameerah said to me, as she handed me the white paper bag with the slices inside.

"Thanks. I'm 'bout to go get the boys and shit. I'll be back."

"Alright. We will wait until you come back to leave."

"Thanks!" I walked out the room and headed to the nurses' station to let them know that I was leaving, but that

Ameerah and Mont were still there. I left and headed to my mom's house. She was watching the kids for us while we were at the hospital. When I pulled into the driveway, I smelled food cooking from outside, and it made my stomach growl loud as hell. I walked inside, and they were sitting with my brother watching movies.

"What you doing here?" He asked me, which made the kids turn around to me.

"Daddy!" They both ran to me yelling.

"Mommy coming?" Mahki asked. I knew he was feeling it with Miyonna not being up and alert since he was a mama's boy.

"Nah. She not here, but I'm going to take you and your brother to see her. You cool with that?"

"Yay! I miss her. I made her a picture since Uncle said that she is sick. She sick, Daddy?"

"Yes. But she resting trying to get better. You want her to get better, right?"

"Yes. I'm ready for her to come home so we can go home." Jr said, and I just nodded.

"Where is your grandma at?" I asked them.

"In the kitchen. She said that we need a good meal." Jr told me, and I let them go back to their movie while I walked in the kitchen.

"You look like shit. You need to go and rest." My mom said, as soon as she looked at me.

"I'm not resting until Mimi wakes up and all this shit is over with." I told her, and she simply shook her head but didn't say anything.

"Well, eat something then." She made a plate and sat it down in front of me. I didn't realize how hungry I was until I ripped the plate and was making another one.

"So, I'm taking the boys to see Mimi. I think this will help her wake up."

"I agree, but if she has all the tubes and shit on her, that's going to scare them then that might not be a good idea."

"It's not that bad."

"Well, okay then." She nodded. I let the kids eat then got them together to go. I even took Princess with me so that she wouldn't be the only kid there with my mom. When we got back to the hospital, I called Ameerah to meet us in the waiting room. When she came in, the boys and I walked out. I held their hands as we walked into the room. When Mahki spotted Mimi, he ran to the bed.

"Mooooommy!" He yelled with a smile on his face. "Mommy, it's me; Mahki."

"She is napping and resting. Talk to her, but don't yell. You have to be quiet in the hospital." I told him.

"Daddy, Mommy is being unresponsive." Mahki said, and I chuckled.

"What that mean, Mahki?" I asked him trying not to laugh at him.

"She not listening to me. That's rude. Why she won't wake up?" He was in his feelings for real.

"She sleeping."

"Fine. Can I kiss her?" He asked with his arms out.

"Yeah. Come on." Picking him up, I walked him closer to the bed then leaned him down. He called himself whispering in her eye. I laughed when he told her to wake up, because he missed her and everyone was being mean to him. My son just didn't like people to tell him no.

"Daddy, are we going home tonight?" Jr. asked.

"Not tonight. Soon, though." I told him, but I wasn't really sure. When Mimi woke up and was cleared to leave the hospital, then we could go home. I wasn't going to tell them that, though.

"Okay. Fine!" Jr snapped at me. I wanted to give his little ass a body shot, but I didn't. I understood him wanting to go home, because I wanted to go home, too. I let them talk to her for a while. I was surprised when Mont and Ameerah walked back in and had Princess with them. I watched as he held her and stood near the bed as she talked to Miyonna. I was hoping anyone could help.

. . .

A few days passed since I brought the boys to the hospital. I guess it helped a little bit, because Miyonna showed some improvement. I was glad that her mother, sister, and brother were coming to see her. Her mom and sister hadn't been to see her since the night that she was shot, and even then, her

146

mother was looking uninterested as if that wasn't her daughter. I didn't see her ass shed one tear, either.

My phone rang, and I walked out the room to answer it when I saw Owen, Tiyonna, and their mother walking towards the room. I just shook my head, because their mother needed to get her mind right. I'm trying to not say anything to her, so I just decided to go in the waiting room until she left. I called my mom to check on the boys, and did a bunch of other shit to just waste time. I ended up dozing off on the couch that was in the waiting room. When I woke up, I saw that an hour and a half had passed, so I got up and headed back to Mimi's room. I popped a mint in my mouth so that I wouldn't have stink breath.

"Where y'all mom at?" I asked Owen and Tiyonna.

"She left. She said that she had to handle something important, so we decided to stay a little longer." Tiyonna said with a shrug.

"Oh. I'm glad she left." I took a seat near the bed. "The doctor or nurse been in here?"

"The nurse came and checked on Mimi. Then, she said for you to page the station when you came back. She said it wasn't that important." Tiyonna said, as she texted away on her phone.

"Alright."

"You think my sister going to die?" she asked, nonchalantly.

"Yo, what is your problem? Why would you even put that out there like that? You wishing for her to die or something?"

"No. Not at all. I'm just asking, because no one tells us anything. Everyone is so hushed about everything. Like, we are not little kids. Why can't we know shit?" She was in her feelings, but I brushed her off. She acted like she didn't fuck with Mimi.

"Ask your mother." Was all I said.

Chapter 13: Monte Washington

Ever since the day that we were at the hospital, and I had the talk with Juelz about the shooting, I had been trying to get everyone together. I finally got ahold of everyone and we were all going to meet up. Ameerah was going to stay at the hospital with Mimi.

While I was handling that for Juelz, I was still trying to figure everything out with Ameerah and the whole baby's mother thing. I hadn't seen or really spoken to Sharanika since I took Princess over to her house. I know that I needed to have a sit down with them both so that was the plan for the day. I was nervous as hell. We were having this talk at my house, and I already knew that, if Ameerah wanted to turn up, then she would.

Ameerah was back home since I walked in on her with dude, but she was staying in a guest room. I was glad that she wasn't fucking with dude like that, though. He was a client even though he asked her on a date. I ain't like that shit, so I had to go and see him. I'm sure he got the hint now. I tried to apologize, but she wasn't really trying to hear it.

Ring. Ring.

I heard the doorbell ring, so I got up to open the door, and Sharanika was standing there with my son. I laughed at her calling herself trying to look good for me. She had on fitted jeans that made her curves really stand out, and she even had makeup on her face. I laughed as I dapped my son up and let them in. Princess came running down the steps.

"Prince! I missed you." She hugged him tightly.

"I missed you, too, little sister. What were you doing?" He asked her.

"Playing. Come play with me." She grabbed his hand and dragged him off.

"Tell your mom to come downstairs, Princess." I told her.

"Okay, Daddy." They went upstairs, and I heard them running through the house. A few seconds later, Ameerah came walking down the steps, so I sat on the couch and she came and sat right next to me. She leaned over and kissed me deeply before smiling at Sharanika. I knew that she was being petty, but I didn't mind, because that was the most affection she given a nigga in so long.

"So, hoe, talk!" She said to Sharanika.

"Our baby daddy called this meeting, so maybe he should talk." She rolled her eyes at Ameerah.

"Chill out, both of y'all! I wanted us to sit down and talk like adults. Ameerah needs to know the truth. Shit, I don't want her thinking that me and you still got something going on. You need to be honest." I told her.

"There isn't anything going on with us anymore, but that don't mean that I don't want it to be something going on. Baby mama privileges…" She said, and Ameerah cut her off.

"Bitch, please!" Ameerah jumped up, and so did I. "You got me fucked up! I wish the fuck you would attempt to throw that rancid ass pussy back on my nigga. Back in the day, I was dumb as hell at first. But when I got smart, your ass caught that golf club. Fucking with me now, you going to catch a bullet. I really don't know what the fuck your ass was thinking when you thought of saying that dumb shit. He used you for your pussy. You got a baby out of it. Congrats to that, but bitch you ain't shit. Fall the fuck back and learn your place." Ameerah went off, as she tried to lunge at Sharanika. Ameerah was making me proud riding for her man.

"Bitch, I know you ain't just say to learn my place. Bitch, we in the same place. We both ain't shit but baby mamas. You don't even have a promise ring, bitch, so get off that high horse you are on."

"I will beat your ass! You trying to justify being a side chick. At the end of the day, Montè Washington is all me. I'm the bitch that he wants to be with. I'm the bitch that he comes home, too. Get used to it. You will never be with him. I'm not about to play with you. You are an old thing that happens to be a baby mama. I'm wifey. Get your shit together!" Ameerah went off on her.

"Whatever!"

"For the record, Ameerah, I just found out about him a few months ago." I pleaded. I wasn't trying to be hit by Ameerah.

"Okay." She simply said.

"Well, aren't y'all just so cute?" Sharanika said, and Ameerah ran up on her. I grabbed her just before she could hit her.

"Man, Sharanika, stop trying to be funny! You need to respect, Ameerah. That's my lady. At the end of the day, you have to deal with her. It's going to be times when she picks Prince up. Plus, that's Princess's brother. Grow the fuck up! I don't want you, and you know it."

"Y'all talking that shit, but she is still a baby mother just like me. She is just a live-in. Y'all need to stop! I'm about to go, though."

"Bye, bitch. I'm about to bond with my stepson, so he can spend a night. Get out!" Ameerah told her.

"Montè, you want me to go?"

"Yeah. Bye!" I told her, before walking in her direction. I walked her to the door with Ameerah on my heels. Sharanika walked out the door talking shit, but I just slammed the door in her face. I turned around and caught a fist to the face. Ameerah rocked my shit.

"I hope you didn't think everything was all good. At the end of the day, you held that shit for a while! Why didn't you tell me? Huh?" She yelled at me.

"Calm down. I didn't know how to tell you."

"How about opening your mouth? That's all you had to do. I guess, I don't mean shit to you. I find it so funny that I been with your black ass for over four years, and we never had not one conversation about our relationship. I hate to say it, but your baby mother was right. I ain't shit but your baby mother. That's crazy, because she was the second person to throw that in my face. It hurts even if I don't show that it does. No, I'm not trying to pressure you into anything, but I'mma ask you this question." She folded her arms. "Do you ever see me as being your wife down the line or soon? Shit, let me know!"

"Man, go ahead with that shit." I didn't know what to say. "Of course I see you as my wife. Why do you care about a piece of paper?"

"Didn't say that I did. I'm asking for effort. Shit, a love contract. A ring. Legally changing my last name. Something besides what it is now. Show appreciation. You have committed a fucking massacre if I wanted to fuck with someone else, but what stepping up have you done? I'm sick of pretending to the world that we are just this one happy ass couple when, behind closed doors, I ain't even really sure about us. Man the fuck up! The streets ain't shit. If you scared of looking like a sucker ass nigga, then let me be, and you go be a man ho." She snapped before turning around and heading up the stairs. I heard the door slam behind her, so I headed down to my basement. I needed to roll up and drink something. My face was throbbing from Ameerah hitting me.

As I sat in my basement, I thought about everything that Ameerah had said, and she was right. I got comfortable with everything that we had going on. She didn't express anything about it, so I didn't either. I guess I should have manned up, because Ameerah was the total package: she was independent, smart, beautiful, a savage in the streets, and she held it down at the crib. She was everything, I wasn't trying to lose her. I had to do something special for her when all this shit cooled down, and Miyonna woke up.

...

It was the day that we were meeting up where our crew be having meetings at. I pulled up at the same time that Juelz did, and we were the first ones to show up. I hoped that they hurried up, because I was ready to make moves. I didn't like the fact that my sis was laid the fuck up in the hospital. It was like everything with her was at a standstill.

"So whatever information we get, we moving on it tonight?" I asked Juelz while we waited.

"It depends. But yo, this is why I fucks with you. You always ready to go." He said, then we dapped up.

"You already know. We been niggas since we were young as fuck. Plus, it's all about Mimi right now. We have to make sure she is straight." I told him.

"Yeah. You right. It's always about her in my world. This shit got me mad as hell, because I knew someone was gunning for her, and said I was going to handle it myself, but I waited too long. I probably should have told her."

"You can't beat yourself up. We know that Mimi a savage out here, but at the end of the day, she is still your wife. You not wrong for not wanting her to worry." I let him know. He shouldn't be blaming himself.

"Man, it's on me, cuz I could have protected her better, especially when she told me that someone was following her. I'm just really ready to get these niggas." He sighed, as everyone started to walk in.

"What's good?" Dun asked. Everyone else sat quietly as if they were waiting for whatever.

"Ain't shit. So, anybody get a tail on Ben or Luther?"

"I have a tail on Ben. I plan on moving in on him. He thinks I want his lame ass." Drea spoke up.

"Word. Add us in on the plan." I told her, and everyone else agreed.

"Alright. I'mma get him alone and knock his ass unconscious, then y'all can come in. I'll make sure that he is all tied up and everything."

"Cool." Juelz told her.

"I got a detail on Luther, but we all need to be in on this, because his old ass got a lot of muthafuckers with him all the time. When we take him out, it's going to be others going out with him. Like a massacre type of thing." Dun chimed in.

"How many people did you count?" Juelz asked him.

"I counted fifteen, but there were a few others. At the same time, I know where he lay his head at, so we should probably strike at night. It be like four guards that rotate shifts and shit."

"So we going to get his ass at night." I looked at him with the 'duh' look.

"He got a lady that be with him. She gotta go, too, because she be practicing shooting and seem like she will lay somebody down over Luther's old ass." Dun informed us.

"I have a question. Why your ass just didn't pop the nigga and the bitch?" Drea asked him. I was kind of wondering the same thing.

"I figured that Juelz wanted to handle that." He snapped at her.

"You right, Dun. I do want to handle that. Good looking." Juelz nodded.

"Word." Dun said. "I feel like shit deeper than what we think. I have a feeling that this is going to uncover some other shit. I got this weird ass feeling about something that I don't want to speak on until I investigate it some more. Then, I will put y'all on to it."

"Shit, like what?" One of Drea's girls asked.

"Some real shit! Let me check more into, then I will let y'all know."

"Alight. Keep us posted."

"I will."

After we had discussed everything, everyone left and went their separate ways. Juelz and I headed to the hospital; I hadn't seen Mimi in a few days.

Chapter 14: Miyonna Pierce-Johnson

All I can think about is the night that I got shot. Everything is still dark and black, but now I can hear voices. The only thing was that they

156

couldn't hear me. I hated to be ignored, and that's how I was feeling at that moment... ignored.

I could hear the conversations that everyone was having. I knew that they were looking for the person that shot me. I just wished I was up so that I could look for the person, too. Maybe I was meant to sit this one out. I had no choice but to lay and listen to everything and everyone.

"Mimi, you need to wake up! We miss you. The kids miss you." I heard Juelz say to me. "The boys been here to see you and talked to you. I wish you could have been able to talk to them." Juelz leaned down and kissed my lips, which felt dry and chapped. I was so embarrassed that he was all on me while I looked like this.

"I am up, bae. I just want to go home." I responded to him but I didn't think he could hear me. When I heard him moving around, I always talk to him; he just never responds. I yell out, yet there's still nothing.

"Babe, you gotta come through, so we can go to an actual doctor's appointment to check on the baby."

"I know baby. I hope it's a girl. I love you." I told him, and there was nothing said. I just felt him holding my hand. Something had to give. I wanted to be heard again. It made me wonder if I was dead and had come back as a ghost. I just laid there fighting hard as hell to open my eyes, but I just couldn't do it. I heard footsteps getting closer to my bed. Someone grabbed my other hand and rubbed on my stomach. It was a loving feeling.

"Miyonna, I wish you wake your light-skinned ass up. Your man and his best friend are touching my last nerves. They got secrets and shit going on around here. I'm ready to fight the both of them." I realized that

157

it was Ameerah talking to me. I missed our conversations. I wondered if she was still dealing with Mont and his bullshit and baby mama mess.

"I'm sorry, Meerah!" I said.

"Goddamit, Miyonna wake your ass up. I'm sick of walking in this bitch and you laid up. Everybody is depressed and shit, because they are worried about you. It really is time to get up. You got me ready to push your ass out this bed. Then, stand you up and make you walk your ass around. It's gon be hood physical therapy. Keep playing with me! WAKE YOUR ASS UP!" Ameerah went off. I wanted to laugh, but I couldn't.

"Shut up, Ameerah! You always talking shit. Sit yo ass down somewhere or something."

"Shut up!" she snapped at Mont. I wanted to jump in the conversation and joke with them, but it was as if I was invisible. I couldn't wait for whatever was wrong to get better.

For everything that was going on, and from listening to what Juelz and the doctors were saying, I guessed that I was pregnant. I wished I was up and running, so that I could enjoy the pregnancy and be in touch with it, but I wasn't. That, along with my kids, made me want to wake up very badly. I was trying and trying, but nothing was happening at all. I just rested my body. I got emotional, because I just wanted to be up and alert for Juelz and my kids.

That's it! Maybe if I just thought about my kids then I could do it.

I thought about Mahki and Jr laughing and playing. I thought about how they would be with their new brother or sister. I thought about how they must have felt coming here and seeing me like this. I thought about how emotional Juelz sounded when he would talk to me about the kids. I thought about how mad I get when I feel like I am being ignored.

After trying and trying, I finally got my eyes open, but the lights hurt them. I blinked a few times, then cried, because I could finally see.

"Oh, shit! She up!" I heard Ameerah yell. Juelz ran near the bed. He kissed me all over the face. He had tears in his eyes, too.

"Bae, I'm glad that you are up. You had me worried as hell." Juelz told me.

"I'm glad you can hear me now." I whispered. My throat was dry as hell, and it kind of burned to talk. I pointed at my throat just as doctors and nurses ran in the room.

"Welcome back, Mrs. Johnson. I know your throat is probably sore. After removing what needs to be removed, we will give you some water." I just nodded my head.

"I'm happy that you are up." Juelz said when the doctors were done and walked out. "I texted Janetta to bring the boys here to see you." I smiled. I was happy that I was going to see them; I missed them. And I was happy when Juelz finally gave me some water. It hurt like hell swallowing it, but the coolness felt good at the same time.

...

I was finally discharged from the hospital, and the first two weeks home, Juelz was up under my ass, waiting on me hand and foot. Then, after them two weeks, his ass got out in the streets. I was happy, in a way, after hearing him on the phone telling someone that, if he had told me that there was a hit on me, I would have been more cautious. He blamed himself, and so did I. I had a bone to pick with his ass, and I was going to wait until he brought his ass in the house before I went to sleep, so that I can address it. I felt like he was avoiding me.

I finally went to a prenatal appointment. Shit, I was surprised that baby girl was still holding on. She was strong as hell. I was going to name her Miracle, because it was a damn miracle that she was still alive. I was happy to be having a girl, though. The boys were happy about that, too. I heard Juelz telling them that they had to protect her at any costs, and I thought that was so cute.

That was a few days ago, and I still hadn't spoken to Juelz, so I was in bed waiting up for him to come home; I was reading a book to keep me up. I looked at the time when I heard the alarm chirp, which told me that he was coming through the door and saw that it was after two in the morning. I kept reading until he got to the doorway of the room. I sat my kindle on the nightstand, as he walked over and kissed me on the lips. I didn't return the kiss, though.

"What you still doing up?" He asked as he undressed.

"I was waiting for you. I don't see too much of you these days. I miss you." I told him, dryly. He looked at me and smiled. Usually, him smiling at me had me ready to fuck him on site, but I didn't feel like that right now.

"Awe, shit. You missed, Daddy?" He asked, as he walked over to his side of the bed and climbed him. He leaned close to me and rubbed my stomach. I pushed his hand away from me.

"What's up? You creeping? You on that shit like your dad? You…" He cut me off.

"The fuck is you talking 'bout? Keep my pops' name out your mouth. I'll never be like that nigga. I ought to beat yo ass for even trying to insinuate that shit. Be lucky that you're pregnant." I rolled my eyes. I didn't give a damn how sensitive he was about the situation with his dad. At the end of the day, I was left in the dark about shit so every option was possible to me.

"You on some bullshit. Why the fuck is you never home?"

"I'm handling shit…" He started to say, but I cut him off again.

"You wouldn't have to handle shit if you would have kept it real with me and let me know that someone was gunning for me."

"Why the fuck would I tell you that shit? So, that you can look over your shoulder all the time? So, that you can be on edge all the time? I want you to live your life normally."

"Obviously, you couldn't do that. You could have at least told Dun. I would have been good. That nigga come through for me all the time."

"The fuck you just say? What do I look like telling another nigga to protect my wife?"

"Obviously, you can't! I have never had this problem until you wanted to hold information and shit!" I got loud. I didn't care no more. I looked at his face and saw that he was hurt ,but I really didn't care. I love Juelz and all that, but he was wrong.

"Really? That's how you feeling?" He asked, and I nodded. I was firm in my thoughts. "If you felt that I couldn't protect you, why are you with me? Why did you marry me? Huh?"

"Because I love you and want to be with you. Let's be honest, though. My street shit has nothing to do with you. That's what Dun is for."

"Fuck that nigga, Dun! You probably fucking him." He said, and I just stared at him. "Cat got your tongue."

"Cat ain't got shit! I'm not fucking him or anyone else." I defended. I have never fucked Dun, but before I was with Juelz, I let Dun taste the kitty. That was way back when Dun was a little nigga on my dad's team. There was a lot of alcohol involved, and I didn't feel bad about it at all.

"Whatever! How about I be out and you call Dun for whatever it is that you need. You pissing me the fuck off with this Dun shit." He said, as he jumped out of bed.

"You mad, huh?" I taunted. He looked at me with a death stare like he was ready to murder my ass, but I didn't care. I was mad as hell, and I felt like he had me fucked up.

"Shut the fuck up, Miyonna! I'm out. I'll be here later on to pick my kids up." He said, as he slipped his Timbs on his feet.

"You not getting shit. My kids chilling right here." I let him know as I got comfortable in the bed.

162

"You really on some shit. I knew that Pocha shit was getting to your head. Let me tell you something, though. I ain't scared of you. I ain't bowing down to shit. The closest I have come to bowing down to your ass is when I got on my knees in the shower and sucked on that pussy. Another thing, you don't want to keep throwing that street shit out there like that, cuz I can make your ass an enemy in these streets and shit will be real. You really don't want them problems, now sleep on what the fuck I just said." He said, then slammed the door behind him. I heard him going down the stairs before I heard the front door close behind him. I laid in the bed comfortably before I finally dozed off.

Waking up the next morning, I felt funny as hell. I didn't know what the feeling was, but I didn't like it. I was glad when Ameerah told me that she was coming to spend the day with me. I got up and headed to the boys' room to check on them, and of course, they were on that damn game playing. I told them to go brush their teeth and wash their faces while I did the same.

When I was done, I headed down to cook breakfast. I would just get dressed after breakfast. I went down and cooked us a good breakfast. After breakfast, we headed upstairs so that we could get dressed. As soon as I stepped out the shower, my doorbell and phone started to ring. I saw that it was Ameerah calling. I answered it and told her where the spare key was outside since I didn't have clothes on. A few minutes later, she walked in the room with Princess on her heels.

"Hi, Teetee. See you later, Teetee." She said then ran down the hall to the boys' room before I could even respond. They loved each other so much and were too cute. All three of them, especially Jr., calls Princess his lil baby.

"What's good, Big 'ems?" Ameerah plopped down on the bed. I grabbed a bra and panty set from the drawer and slipped them on before pulling the towel off me. I grabbed a long-sleeve jumper to throw on and my slippers. I wasn't going anywhere.

"What's up?" I asked her as I sat down.

"I want to ask you a question, but I want you to be honest with me, because I'm sick of the whispers." She looked at me in my eyes.

"What's going on?"

"Are you a hitman?" She boldly asked.

"No." I answered. She looked at me like I was lying. I might as well just tell her the truth. "I'm not a hitman. I'm a connect, Meerah. Juelz and them buy from me. As well as other niggas." I told her, and her mouth dropped.

"I thought we were best friends. How come you never told me?" She asked, sadly.

"I separate being a connect from being a mom and all that. When I do that, no one calls me Miyonna or Mimi; they call me Pocha. I didn't tell you, because I consider you as being a part of my home life. Being a connect is the reason why me and my mother do not get along. She thinks that it's a man's job, and she hates that my dad passed it down to me when he died, but it was inevitable, because I was the oldest child and next in line."

"My feelings are kind of hurt, because you never told me." She was in her feelings. I really didn't feel that bad, though.

"I have a motto about the way I live my life now, Meerah. I say, a lady in the streets and a savage in the streets."

"What does that even mean?" I couldn't believe we were really having this talk.

"It means that, at home, I am like every other female. I let my emotions show, I cry, I'm lovey dovey with my man. You know. But when I'm out in the streets, I go hard. I push my feelings to the side and show no emotion. I just handle my business."

"Oh. I feel like I barely know you, which is weird since I knew you since we were damn near babies."

"It's really not that deep, Ameerah."

"To me it is, because you kept all this from me for years. What about Drea and them?"

"They are hitmen. They are a team of hit women that work for me."

"OH MY FUCKING GOSH! I CAN'T BELIEVE YOU HAD ME HANGING AROUND FEMALE SERIAL KILLERS!" She yelled jumping up. She started to pace, and I had to calm her down.

165

"Relax, Ameerah. They know when to turn up and when to turn down."

"Thank God we all got along or else my ass could be floating in somebody's sewer right now. I could really be stinking." I chuckled, because she was overreacting. "It's not funny, Mimi. You put my life in danger." Was she getting mad?

"Are you serious right now?"

"I'm dead ass serious."

"Wow!" was all I said. I was going to give her the little moment that she wanted. I was not about to play with her.

"Don't wow me."

"I am wowing you. Nobody was really thinking about your ass. They work for me, meaning that they only make moves like that when I give them the go. That night, we were all chilling. Not in street mode. You over there doing the most. You are my best friend, and I would never let anything happen to you, so shut up and calm down!" I told her, and I saw her face soften up.

"I guess you are right."

"I know I am."

"Okay. How are you and Juelz?" She asked, and I rolled my eyes before running the story down of everything that happened. When I was done, she had her mouth dropped. "Mimi, you were wrong. You better be lucky that Ju not one of them soft made niggas, because if he was, that would have made him want to commit suicide. Why would you throw another dude in his face?"

"It's the truth, Ameerah. I never had beef like this where someone was gunning for me. The other time I had beef like this Dun knew, then we handled it. It didn't make it this far where I'm sitting with bullet wounds after being in the hospital for over a month."

"You still was wrong. No matter how you try and justify it. At the end of the day, he is your husband."

"When I first started this, we agreed that he would stay out of my street shit. If he would have stuck to that, none of this would have happened. But whatever, it happened, and Dun is fixing everything. Enough about me, what's going on with you and Mont?" I asked her.

"While you were in the hospital, we had a sit-down with his baby mama. Let's just say that it created other problems." She ran the story down to me about what happened and what his baby mother said about Ameerah being a baby mother too except she was a live-in. I could tell that Ameerah was hurt like hell just by the facial expressions that she was making while she told the story.

"So you talked to Mont about what the bitch said after she left?"

"Yes. You know how I am. I don't put our business out there like that. I acted like we were this perfect ride or die couple, but when she left, I said what I had to say. I don't know if our relationship is going to last or not. We been together for almost five years, and all I am to him is the mother of his child and girlfriend. We not getting any younger, and it's like he has no plans of our relationship going to another level. I'm not saying marriage, but can a girl get at least a promise ring or something? Like, some kind of effort to show that you have some type of plans for us."

"Damn. I feel you, though. Pray on it. Prayer won't steer you wrong. If it's meant to be, then it will be." I said, when I noticed that she had tears in her eyes. I knew that Meerah loved Mont deeply. They had been through too much together. Cheating, break-ups, and now, baby mamas. It was going to get better, if she was with him or not.

"Thank you, Mimi."

"You're welcome. So, you and him still living together?"

"Yeah. I went back home, but it's weird as hell. We have sex, but we sleep in different rooms. I know that Princess is wondering what is going on, but I really don't know what to do. I want to be with him forever, but I don't want to be with him forever and unhappy."

"You deserve happiness. Everyone does. It will all work out. Trust me."

"I hope so, but while you talking about me, you should apologize to Juelz. He was just trying to protect you. At the end of the day, he is your husband, you are pregnant, and y'all already have two kids together. Y'all have more at stake."

"I'm not apologizing, especially since he owes me one."

"You are being petty. That's why he walked out on you. He came to the house and told Mont that he was leaving until you get your mind right. He said that you really bugging. Nigga had his ring off and everything. I was peeking around the corner when they were in the kitchen talking." She told me.

"Oh, really! Cool." I didn't even know what to say. I was kind of speechless.

"You okay?"

"Yeah. I need to focus on me and this pregnancy. The baby's kind of small for me to be about five months, so I'm not about to stress myself out."

"Right. The baby is more important."

"Way more. So, what are you naming the baby?"

"Well, I found out that it is a girl, so I'm going to name her Miracle Jaylah Johnson. I mean, she is a miracle that happened being that I was in a whole coma or whatever you call it, and she still survived."

"Wait, why did you say or whatever?"

"I don't know what a coma is supposed to be like, but when y'all were visiting me in the hospital and talking to me, I could hear everything that y'all were saying, and I even tried to respond, but I guess y'all couldn't hear me. It was weird as hell, but I don't think it was really a coma."

"Wow. That's crazy. But what you got that we can cook? I need a good meal."

Andrea

"I been having a taste for some fried barbecue chicken, homemade garlic mashed potatoes, buttery corn, plantains, and cornbread." I said with my eyes closed picturing the meal in front of me.

"Well, damn! You going to have an orgasm over it?" She asked me.

"I might." I joked with her.

"Come on. Let's go cook. That's something fun we can do since it's been a while." After checking on the kids, we headed downstairs to the kitchen. It felt like old times hanging with my bestie. The only thing missing was our men in the basement doing whatever it is that they do down there while they wait for the food to be done. Maybe, one day, we would get back to that.

Chapter 14: Miyonna Pierce- Johnson

All I can think about is the night that I got shot. Everything is still dark and black, but now I can hear voices. The only thing was that they couldn't hear me. I hated to be ignored, and that's how I was feeling at that moment... ignored.

I could hear the conversations that everyone was having. I knew that they were looking for the person that shot me. I just wished I was up so that I could look for the person, too. Maybe I was meant to sit this one out. I had no choice but to lay and listen to everything and everyone.

"Mimi, you need to wake up! We miss you. The kids miss you." I heard Juelz say to me. "The boys been here to see you and talked to you. I wish you could have been able to talk to them." Juelz leaned down and kissed my lips, which felt dry and chapped. I was so embarrassed that he was all on me while I looked like this.

"I am up, bae. I just want to go home." I responded to him but I didn't think he could hear me. When I heard him moving around, I always talk to him; he just never responds. I yell out, yet there's still nothing.

"Babe, you gotta come through, so we can go to an actual doctor's appointment to check on the baby."

"I know baby. I hope it's a girl. I love you." I told him, and there was nothing said. I just felt him holding my hand. Something had to give. I wanted to be heard again. It made me wonder if I was dead and had come back as a ghost. I just laid there fighting hard as hell to open my

eyes, but I just couldn't do it. I heard footsteps getting closer to my bed. Someone grabbed my other hand and rubbed on my stomach. It was a loving feeling.

"Miyonna, I wish you wake your light-skinned ass up. Your man and his best friend are touching my last nerves. They got secrets and shit going on around here. I'm ready to fight the both of them." I realized that it was Ameerah talking to me. I missed our conversations. I wondered if she was still dealing with Mont and his bullshit and baby mama mess.

"I'm sorry, Meerah!" I said.

"Goddamit, Miyonna wake your ass up. I'm sick of walking in this bitch and you laid up. Everybody is depressed and shit, because they are worried about you. It really is time to get up. You got me ready to push your ass out this bed. Then, stand you up and make you walk your ass around. It's gon be hood physical therapy. Keep playing with me! WAKE YOUR ASS UP!" Ameerah went off. I wanted to laugh, but I couldn't.

"Shut up, Ameerah! You always talking shit. Sit yo ass down somewhere or something."

"Shut up!" she snapped at Mont. I wanted to jump in the conversation and joke with them, but it was as if I was invisible. I couldn't wait for whatever was wrong to get better.

For everything that was going on, and from listening to what Juelz and the doctors were saying, I guessed that I was pregnant. I wished I was up and running, so that I could enjoy the pregnancy and be in touch with it, but I wasn't. That, along with my kids, made me want to wake up very badly. I was trying and trying, but nothing was happening at all.

a Lady in the Sheets, A Savage in the Streets

I just rested my body. I got emotional, because I just wanted to be up and alert for Juelz and my kids.

That's it! Maybe if I just thought about my kids then I could do it.

I thought about Mahki and Jr laughing and playing. I thought about how they would be with their new brother or sister. I thought about how they must have felt coming here and seeing me like this. I thought about how emotional Juelz sounded when he would talk to me about the kids. I thought about how mad I get when I feel like I am being ignored.

After trying and trying, I finally got my eyes open, but the lights hurt them. I blinked a few times, then cried, because I could finally see.

"Oh, shit! She up!" I heard Ameerah yell. Juelz ran near the bed. He kissed me all over the face. He had tears in his eyes, too.

"Bae, I'm glad that you are up. You had me worried as hell." Juelz told me.

"I'm glad you can hear me now." I whispered. My throat was dry as hell, and it kind of burned to talk. I pointed at my throat just as doctors and nurses ran in the room.

"Welcome back, Mrs. Johnson. I know your throat is probably sore. After removing what needs to be removed, we will give you some water." I just nodded my head.

"I'm happy that you are up." Juelz said when the doctors were done and walked out. "I texted Janetta to bring the boys here to see you." I smiled. I was happy that I was going to see them; I missed them. And I was happy when Juelz finally gave me some water. It hurt like hell swallowing it, but the coolness felt good at the same time.

Andrea

...

I was finally discharged from the hospital, and the first two weeks home, Juelz was up under my ass, waiting on me hand and foot. Then, after them two weeks, his ass got out in the streets. I was happy, in a way, after hearing him on the phone telling someone that, if he had told me that there was a hit on me, I would have been more cautious. He blamed himself, and so did I. I had a bone to pick with his ass, and I was going to wait until he brought his ass in the house before I went to sleep, so that I can address it. I felt like he was avoiding me.

I finally went to a prenatal appointment. Shit, I was surprised that baby girl was still holding on. She was strong as hell. I was going to name her Miracle, because it was a damn miracle that she was still alive. I was happy to be having a girl, though. The boys were happy about that, too. I heard Juelz telling them that they had to protect her at any costs, and I thought that was so cute.

That was a few days ago, and I still hadn't spoken to Juelz, so I was in bed waiting up for him to come home; I was reading a book to keep me up. I looked at the time when I heard the alarm chirp, which told me that he was coming through the door and saw that it was after two in the morning. I kept reading until he got to the doorway of the room. I sat my kindle on the nightstand, as he walked over and kissed me on the lips. I didn't return the kiss, though.

"What you still doing up?" He asked as he undressed.

"I was waiting for you. I don't see too much of you these days. I miss you." I told him, dryly. He looked at me and smiled. Usually, him smiling at me had me ready to fuck him on site, but I didn't feel like that right now.

"Awe, shit. You missed, Daddy?" He asked, as he walked over to his side of the bed and climbed him. He leaned close to me and rubbed my stomach. I pushed his hand away from me.

"What's up? You creeping? You on that shit like your dad? You..." He cut me off.

"The fuck is you talking 'bout? Keep my pops' name out your mouth. I'll never be like that nigga. I ought to beat yo ass for even trying to insinuate that shit. Be lucky that you're pregnant." I rolled my eyes. I didn't give a damn how sensitive he was about the situation with his dad. At the end of the day, I was left in the dark about shit so every option was possible to me.

"You on some bullshit. Why the fuck is you never home?"

"I'm handling shit..." He started to say, but I cut him off again.

"You wouldn't have to handle shit if you would have kept it real with me and let me know that someone was gunning for me."

"Why the fuck would I tell you that shit? So, that you can look over your shoulder all the time? So, that you can be on edge all the time? I want you to live your life normally."

"Obviously, you couldn't do that. You could have at least told Dun. I would have been good. That nigga come through for me all the time."

"The fuck you just say? What do I look like telling another nigga to protect my wife?"

"Obviously, you can't! I have never had this problem until you wanted to hold information and shit!" I got loud. I didn't care no more. I looked at his face and saw that he was hurt ,but I really didn't care. I love Juelz and all that, but he was wrong.

"Really? That's how you feeling?" He asked, and I nodded. I was firm in my thoughts. "If you felt that I couldn't protect you, why are you with me? Why did you marry me? Huh?"

"Because I love you and want to be with you. Let's be honest, though. My street shit has nothing to do with you. That's what Dun is for."

"Fuck that nigga, Dun! You probably fucking him." He said, and I just stared at him. "Cat got your tongue."

"Cat ain't got shit! I'm not fucking him or anyone else." I defended. I have never fucked Dun, but before I was with Juelz, I let Dun taste the kitty. That was way back when Dun was a little nigga on my dad's team. There was a lot of alcohol involved, and I didn't feel bad about it at all.

"Whatever! How about I be out and you call Dun for whatever it is that you need. You pissing me the fuck off with this Dun shit." He said, as he jumped out of bed.

"You mad, huh?" I taunted. He looked at me with a death stare like he was ready to murder my ass, but I didn't care. I was mad as hell, and I felt like he had me fucked up.

"Shut the fuck up, Miyonna! I'm out. I'll be here later on to pick my kids up." He said, as he slipped his Timbs on his feet.

"You not getting shit. My kids chilling right here." I let him know as I got comfortable in the bed.

"You really on some shit. I knew that Pocha shit was getting to your head. Let me tell you something, though. I ain't scared of you. I ain't bowing down to shit. The closest I have come to bowing down to your ass is when I got on my knees in the shower and sucked on that pussy. Another thing, you don't want to keep throwing that street shit out there like that, cuz I can make your ass an enemy in these streets and shit will be real. You really don't want them problems, now sleep on what the fuck I just said." He said, then slammed the door behind him. I heard him going down the stairs before I heard the front door close behind him. I laid in the bed comfortably before I finally dozed off.

Waking up the next morning, I felt funny as hell. I didn't know what the feeling was, but I didn't like it. I was glad when Ameerah told me that she was coming to spend the day with me. I got up and headed to the boys' room to check on them, and of course, they were on that damn game playing. I told them to go brush their teeth and wash their faces while I did the same.

Andrea

When I was done, I headed down to cook breakfast. I would just get dressed after breakfast. I went down and cooked us a good breakfast. After breakfast, we headed upstairs so that we could get dressed. As soon as I stepped out the shower, my doorbell and phone started to ring. I saw that it was Ameerah calling. I answered it and told her where the spare key was outside since I didn't have clothes on. A few minutes later, she walked in the room with Princess on her heels.

"Hi, Teetee. See you later, Teetee." She said then ran down the hall to the boys' room before I could even respond. They loved each other so much and were too cute. All three of them, especially Jr., calls Princess his lil baby.

"What's good, Big 'ems?" Ameerah plopped down on the bed. I grabbed a bra and panty set from the drawer and slipped them on before pulling the towel off me. I grabbed a long-sleeve jumper to throw on and my slippers. I wasn't going anywhere.

"What's up?" I asked her as I sat down.

"I want to ask you a question, but I want you to be honest with me, because I'm sick of the whispers." She looked at me in my eyes.

"What's going on?"

"Are you a hitman?" She boldly asked.

"No." I answered. She looked at me like I was lying. I might as well just tell her the truth. "I'm not a hitman. I'm a connect, Meerah. Juelz and them buy from me. As well as other niggas." I told her, and her mouth dropped.

"I thought we were best friends. How come you never told me?" She asked, sadly.

"I separate being a connect from being a mom and all that. When I do that, no one calls me Miyonna or Mimi; they call me Pocha. I didn't tell you, because I consider you as being a part of my home life. Being a connect is the reason why me and my mother do not get along. She thinks that it's a man's job, and she hates that my dad passed it down to me when he died, but it was inevitable, because I was the oldest child and next in line."

"My feelings are kind of hurt, because you never told me." She was in her feelings. I really didn't feel that bad, though.

"I have a motto about the way I live my life now, Meerah. I say, a lady in the streets and a savage in the streets."

"What does that even mean?" I couldn't believe we were really having this talk.

"It means that, at home, I am like every other female. I let my emotions show, I cry, I'm lovey dovey with my man. You know. But when I'm out in the streets, I go hard. I push my feelings to the side and show no emotion. I just handle my business."

"Oh. I feel like I barely know you, which is weird since I knew you since we were damn near babies."

"It's really not that deep, Ameerah."

"To me it is, because you kept all this from me for years. What about Drea and them?"

"They are hitmen. They are a team of hit women that work for me."

"OH MY FUCKING GOSH! I CAN'T BELIEVE YOU HAD ME HANGING AROUND FEMALE SERIAL KILLERS!" She yelled jumping up. She started to pace, and I had to calm her down.

"Relax, Ameerah. They know when to turn up and when to turn down."

"Thank God we all got along or else my ass could be floating in somebody's sewer right now. I could really be stinking." I chuckled, because she was overreacting. "It's not funny, Mimi. You put my life in danger." Was she getting mad?

"Are you serious right now?"

"I'm dead ass serious."

"Wow!" was all I said. I was going to give her the little moment that she wanted. I was not about to play with her.

"Don't wow me."

"I am wowing you. Nobody was really thinking about your ass. They work for me, meaning that they only make moves like that when I give them the go. That night, we were all chilling. Not in street mode. You over there doing the most. You are my best friend, and I would never let anything happen to you, so shut up and calm down!" I told her, and I saw her face soften up.

"I guess you are right."

"I know I am."

"Okay. How are you and Juelz?" She asked, and I rolled my eyes before running the story down of everything that happened. When I was done, she had her mouth dropped. "Mimi, you were wrong. You better be lucky that Ju not one of them soft made niggas, because if he was, that would have made him want to commit suicide. Why would you throw another dude in his face?"

"It's the truth, Ameerah. I never had beef like this where someone was gunning for me. The other time I had beef like this Dun knew, then we handled it. It didn't make it this far where I'm sitting with bullet wounds after being in the hospital for over a month."

"You still was wrong. No matter how you try and justify it. At the end of the day, he is your husband."

"When I first started this, we agreed that he would stay out of my street shit. If he would have stuck to that, none of this would have happened. But whatever, it happened, and Dun is fixing everything. Enough about me, what's going on with you and Mont?" I asked her.

"While you were in the hospital, we had a sit-down with his baby mama. Let's just say that it created other problems." She ran the story down to me about what happened and what his baby mother said about Ameerah being a baby mother too except she was a live-in. I could tell that Ameerah was hurt like hell just by the facial expressions that she was making while she told the story.

"So you talked to Mont about what the bitch said after she left?"

"Yes. You know how I am. I don't put our business out there like that. I acted like we were this perfect ride or die couple, but when she left, I said what I had to say. I don't know if our relationship is going to last or not. We been together for almost five years, and all I am to him is the mother of his child and girlfriend. We not getting any younger, and it's like he has no plans of our relationship going to another level. I'm not saying marriage, but can a girl get at least a promise ring or something? Like, some kind of effort to show that you have some type of plans for us."

"Damn. I feel you, though. Pray on it. Prayer won't steer you wrong. If it's meant to be, then it will be." I said, when I noticed that she had tears in her eyes. I knew that Meerah loved Mont deeply. They had been through too much together. Cheating, break-ups, and now, baby mamas. It was going to get better, if she was with him or not.

"Thank you, Mimi."

"You're welcome. So, you and him still living together?"

"Yeah. I went back home, but it's weird as hell. We have sex, but we sleep in different rooms. I know that Princess is wondering what is going on, but I really don't know what to do. I want to be with him forever, but I don't want to be with him forever and unhappy."

"You deserve happiness. Everyone does. It will all work out. Trust me."

"I hope so, but while you talking about me, you should apologize to Juelz. He was just trying to protect you. At the end of the day, he is your husband, you are pregnant, and y'all already have two kids together. Y'all have more at stake."

"I'm not apologizing, especially since he owes me one."

"You are being petty. That's why he walked out on you. He came to the house and told Mont that he was leaving until you get your mind right. He said that you really bugging. Nigga had his ring off and everything. I was peeking around the corner when they were in the kitchen talking." She told me.

"Oh, really! Cool." I didn't even know what to say. I was kind of speechless.

"You okay?"

"Yeah. I need to focus on me and this pregnancy. The baby's kind of small for me to be about five months, so I'm not about to stress myself out."

"Right. The baby is more important."

"Way more. So, what are you naming the baby?"

"Well, I found out that it is a girl, so I'm going to name her Miracle Jaylah Johnson. I mean, she is a miracle that happened being that I was in a whole coma or whatever you call it, and she still survived."

"Wait, why did you say or whatever?"

"I don't know what a coma is supposed to be like, but when y'all were visiting me in the hospital and talking to me, I could hear everything that y'all were saying, and I even tried to respond, but I guess y'all couldn't hear me. It was weird as hell, but I don't think it was really a coma."

"Wow. That's crazy. But what you got that we can cook? I need a good meal."

"I been having a taste for some fried barbecue chicken, homemade garlic mashed potatoes, buttery corn, plantains, and cornbread." I said with my eyes closed picturing the meal in front of me.

"Well, damn! You going to have an orgasm over it?" She asked me.

"I might." I joked with her.

"Come on. Let's go cook. That's something fun we can do since it's been a while." After checking on the kids, we headed downstairs to the kitchen. It felt like old times hanging with my bestie. The only thing missing was our men in the basement doing whatever it is that they do down there while they wait for the food to be done. Maybe, one day, we would get back to that.

Chapter 15: Juelz Johnson

Miyonna really had some shit with her. She really was talking big shit like Dun was *that* nigga. If he was, then he would have some real shit going for himself besides being a right-hand man. I ain't jealous of the nigga by a longshot. The thing I don't like is that she threw that shit in my face. Like I was less than a grown ass nigga. I never came as close as I did to putting my hands on her. When she was spitting that bullshit, I balled my fists up ready to rock her shit. The only thing that kept me from laying that ass out was the fact that I loved her, and she was pregnant, so I had to walk away before I went the fuck off.

I headed to my nigga Mont's house, because he was the only person that understood the situation and would be real about everything without being biased. That's crazy that I couldn't go to my pops, cuz that nigga wanna be a bitch fucking with another nigga. I know he wanted to talk to me about the shit that happened with my mother, but I'm good on that. I'm not a homophobe at all, but I'm not sitting up listening to him tell me how he in love with another nigga. Nope, not about to happen, especially with everything else that I have going on.

When I got to Mont's house, we sat in the living room smoking while I told him what was up. He looked at me with a shocked expression. He knew what was up. When it was all said and done, I wanted to go and pull up on Dun. After being there for a while, I left and headed to this hideout apartment that I had.

Sitting on the couch, all I could do was think of the chain of events that had happened. It was crazy that, just a few weeks before all of this, I was worried about Mimi because she was shot the fuck up. Then, she finally woke up and was in the hospital for a week before she could go home. When she finally gets home, I wait on her ass hand and foot for two whole weeks, only for her to turn around and act like she wasn't appreciative of it. That shit had me pissed the fuck off, because I knew that, as her husband, I was doing the right thing, but right now, I'm at the point of saying fuck her. I'mma let her get her mind right. The only two reasons I want to hear from her is when it's about the boys and when she goes into labor. I really didn't have much else to say to her.

I went over and over in my head how I was going to approach Dun. I didn't him to think I was playing with his ass, but at the same time, I didn't want him to think I was all cool and shit with him. By the time I thought everything through, I had dozed off on the couch.

Waking up the next morning, I handled my hygiene before grabbing my shit and heading out the door. I was going to pick my kids up and take them to breakfast, but when I made it to the house, I got mad as hell when I went to use my key in the door, but it didn't work. *I know damn well she didn't change the goddam locks.* I started pressing the doorbell and knocking on the door rudely. She really had me fucked up beyond belief. When she opened the door, I grabbed her by the throat and pushed her inside. Throwing her against the wall, I got close to her face.

"What the fuck is wrong with you? Why the fuck would you change the fucking locks?" I asked, as I squeezed tighter.

"Why do you care? You walked out like you was saying fuck us." She rolled her eyes, and that made me even madder. She was pissing me off. I squeezed her throat tighter. I didn't realize it was that tight until I saw her eyes roll in the back of her head and her skin started turning colors. I let go, but my eyes were trained on her. "Are you fucking serious right now? You really tried to fucking kill me? Get the fuck out!"

"I wish I would. You really been testing me, and I been letting it slide. I'm not letting it slide no more. Get yourself together. Respect me!"

"You ain't even a real man. Anyway, why are you here?" She said, as she rubbed her neck looking at me.

"I came to get my kids to take them out. Don't fucking question me! Go sit and rub your stomach or something."

"Don't talk to me like that!"

"Shut the fuck up! I gotta talk to you like this, cuz you don't appreciate my gentleman side. Now, sit the fuck down like I said. Stop playing with me!" I snapped at her, and she sat down. I grilled her before walking away and heading up the stairs. I walked in the boys' room, and they were up.

"Daddy!" Mahki jumped on me. I hugged him. "You mad at mommy?" He asked, and I didn't know what to say.

"No. I'm not."

"Why you was yelling at her then?" Jr chimed in and asked.

"Don't worry about it. Did y'all get in the bath already?"

"Yes. We just need to get dressed, but I wanted to play my game."

"Alright. Let's get y'all dressed so we can go out." I told them, as I put Mahki down and walked towards the closet. I quickly grabbed both of them an outfit. They got dressed as I went back in and grabbed their black Timbs.

Ten minutes later, they were dressed, and we were walking down the stairs then out the door. Mimi was still sitting on the couch like she was waiting for me to say something to her, but she had me fucked up. I wasn't saying shit to her ass. After getting the boys in the car, we headed to Perkins. Of course, the boys talked my head off all the way there, and after we had sat down, but I didn't mind. I was only away from them for a day, but I missed them. They were being their normal self, so I wasn't prepared when Jr asked me what he did.

"What did you say?" I asked him.

"I said, are you and mommy getting divorced?" He asked again.

"What you know about divorces? Where you learned that from?" I asked him.

"They talk about it in school. Then, I asked them what it was, and they told me everything about it."

"Wow."

"Yup. You don't learn if you don't ask questions. Right?" He asked.

"You're right."

"So, are you and mommy getting a divorce or not?" He asked, and I wanted to know why he was so pressed about divorces.

"No. We are not. Why you so intrigued by it?"

"Because I heard Auntie Meerah say that you said that you were moving out. Then, you really didn't come home, so I put it together. You and mommy were arguing today, too, so I just thought that you were." He told me with a sure look.

"No. Grown-ups argue sometimes. It will be okay." I told him while cursing myself. I never wanted to act like that in front of my kids or where they could hear shit.

"Okay." He went back to eating.

"I want to apologize to you and Mahki, because I never wanted y'all to hear me and Mommy arguing. That's not cool, so I apologize."

"It's okay." He told me, and I dapped the both of them up. We enjoyed the rest of breakfast together, before I asked them what they wanted to do for the day. I was going to roll up on Dun's ass, but I changed my mind and was just going to wait for the opportunity to present itself. After the boys had said that they wanted to go to R-bounce, that's where we headed. As soon as we got there, they took their shoes off and handed them to me before taking off. It wasn't really anyone

189

in there, but I guess that was because it was before noon. I took a seat at the table, then felt my phone vibrating. I pulled it out and saw it was back to back text messages from Miyonna.

Wife: you really choked me, though!

Wife: I hate you right now. I swear to god I do.

Wife: I'm going to the hospital.

Wife: you should be lucky ain't no snitching in my blood.

I just simply ignored her texts as I called Ameerah. When she answered, I told her to keep me posted on everything that they said. After she had got smart a few times, she agreed. I probably looked dumb as fuck for not going with my pregnant wife, but I couldn't deal with her mouth right now. I sat back chilling while the boys ran around having fun for most of the day. By the time we were leaving, it was well in the afternoon.

"Daddy, we had fun. Where we going now?" Mahki asked, as we walked to the car. His little ass was just too excited. Jr was quiet as hell, so I wanted to talk to his little ass. He was too quiet for my liking.

"Where you want to go?" I asked him.

"Home. So we all can play the game. You going to play with us, Daddy?" Mahki asked.

"Yeah."

"Yay!   Come on. You gotta speed so that we can get there fast in a hurry." Mahki told me from the backseat. Jr and I fell out laughing. Mahki was animated. On my way to the house, I called Miyonna to see if she was at the house. She said that she was, and I hung up. Wasn't no need to stay on the phone when I was about to pull up.

When we pulled up, I saw Ameerah's car in the driveway. I helped the boys out the car before we walked to the door. Forgetting that fast that Miyonna's petty ass changed the locks, I rang the doorbell with an attitude. Ameerah opened the door with a confused look on her face.

"What you ringing the bell for?"

"Miyonna had the locks changed. Where she at?"

"Upstairs. She on bedrest." She said, and I headed for the steps. I marched up the steps to our bedroom. I walked in, and she was laying on the bed in just bra and panties. Her baby bump was on display, but I ignored all that.

"I'm sick of repeating this shit so this is my last time saying this shit." She just looked at me. "You need to go back to old Miyonna, because you taking this Pocha shit to the head. You doing too much. You wanna be on that bullshit, then we can get a damn divorce. I'm not dealing with the bullshit. It's enough shit going on. Get your shit together. You wanna be a nigga?"

"What you talking about?"

"I'm talking about you acting like you the one walking around swinging dick. I'm sick of the shit. You wanna swing dick, let me know, so I can be on my way. Then, you can buy all the dick you want and find a bitch, cuz ain't no real nigga gon be with the shits."

Andrea

"Whatever!"

"Yeah. Whatever! Give me a fucking key to the house. Change another lock if you want to. I'm changing my whole approach with your ass. I'm not playing with your ass." I let her know.

"You found balls!"

"Been had them. It was a lot going on, so I let your ass slide, but that's all dead now. Keep fucking with me." I barked at her, and she looked spooked. I didn't care though.

"Okay."

"So, what the doctor say?"

"My blood pressure was high. They wanted to keep me, but I signed myself out, so they told me to be on bedrest."

"Alright. I'mma stay here to take care of the boys. I'll sleep in a guestroom." I walked out the room and headed to hang with the boys. We stayed in the room for a while playing the game. I looked at the time and saw that it was going on dinner time so I was about to go and see what Miyonna wanted to eat. I got closer to the bedroom and heard her and Ameerah talking.

"Meerah, I think I went too far this time. Juelz is tired of me."

"I wouldn't be me if I didn't keep it real with you. So, I'm going to ask you this… can you blame him?"

"I'm just frustrated with the shooting and shit. Then, the shit with my mom. It's just annoying." Miyonna said with emotion like she was crying.

"Don't you think that should push y'all together instead of you pulling apart?"

"I guess, but who are you to talk? You talking 'bout leaving Mont for real?" Miyonna said, and I was shocked. I pulled my phone and started recording their conversation. I was going to let my boy hear this shit.

"It's different. You have more at stake, Miyonna. You are that man's wife and you're pregnant. You invested more. It's a different league. I'm just a live-in baby mama. I can walk away without the extra. We only have one child." She said, sadly. "Feel me!"

"Yeah. Don't cry."

"I can't help it. You don't know how it feels to think that you love someone more than they love you. Especially, when you been with them for years catching deeper feelings as times go on. Then, to top it off, you fake to the world that everything is all good, but behind closed doors, it's totally different. Secret kids popping up and shit."

"Everything going to be okay. Trust me."

"I want to walk away, but I don't want to be weak. At the same time, I don't barely say too much to him, and we don't stay in the same room. Sometimes I feel childish as hell, but then again, I need to re-evaluate everything. I don't know. My thoughts are all over the place."

"You got this. It will get better. Either way." I had listened to enough. Miyonna was in no position to be giving advice. I stopped recording and slipped my phone in my pocket before walking in the room with them.

"What you want to eat for dinner?" I asked Miyonna, and she looked at me as if to say that I had the nerve to be interrupting her.

"I want baked ziti. I been having a taste for it." She said.

"Alright. I'll order it from Bellas. You want bread or salad with it?"

"Salad with extra olives and Italian dressing." She closed her eyes and let out a moan. My dick jumped, and it was my cue to walk out the room.

"Alright, man." I walked back to the boys' room, then called and ordered the food.

. . .

I was chilling when I got the call from one of my boys that they got that nigga Vin, so I jumped up and hurried out the door to my car. Hopping in, I sped off to where they were holding him at. When I got there, I left my important shit in the car and grabbed my piece. Nigga was dying after he gave me the shit I needed to know. I walked in and grabbed a garbage bag before walking near dude. I ripped it so I could put it on like Missy Elliot did in her video. I ain't want no splatter on me. I walked near everyone and saw that it was Drea and her girls as well as niggas from my crew. I saw that Dun was there, too, but I brushed him off so I could handle my shit. Grabbing a chair, I pulled it up to Vin's face. He was tied to a chair.

"What's good, little homie?" His eyes got big as hell. "You like shooting people and shit. I just want to know why."

"Man, who I shoot? What I do?" He asked like he was a small child.

"So about a month or so ago, you don't remember shooting a lady that was about to step in a taxi?" I asked him.

"Oh, you talking about Pocha? Yeah, I was there." He was starting to get bold. He actually had a small smirk on his face.

"Yeah, her. Now, what did she to you that made you shoot her?"

"She didn't do nothing to me. I got paid a nice amount to pop her so I did. It was business. I usually ain't a killer, but that two hundred and fifty thousand dollars changed my mind." He smiled.

"Well, whoever paid you, you need to give them their money back, cuz baby girl still alive. She kicked back chilling after surviving that punk shit that you had flying." His face dropped. "Thought you offed her, huh?"

"Man, whatever, you just saying that!"

"I'm not. But more importantly, who paid you to do that shit?"

"Oh, wouldn't you like to know?" He laughed. I looked at Mont, and he nodded at me. "I ain't a snitch, so I'm not saying shit."

"Word?" I asked with raised eyebrow. Mont walked over to me and handed me a butcher knife. I made sure he burned the cutting part. I used it and came down on Vin's fingers.

"Fuuuuuuuck!" He yelled out! I chuckled.

"You going to tell me now?"

"Nope! Fuck you, nigga!" He said to me, and I nodded. Drea walked over and stabbed him in his knees twice.

"Still not talking?" Drea chuckled.

"Stupid bitch!" He spat at Drea making her step back. "This shit is burning. Fuck is wrong with y'all? You said ole girl not dead so why y'all here torturing me? Ahhh, fuck!"

"Watch your mouth! Say one more thing, and your top gon' be missing next." Drea snapped at him. She had quickly taken the knife to his top lip. Shit, I blinked and almost missed the shit happening. I had to move back when she tossed the lip back.

"Damn, girl. Fuck the fact that we all sitting here behind you." I said to her, and she chuckled.

"My bad. I forgot. I was in my zone." She said.

"It's cool." I let her know. "Now, lil nigga, you gon say a name now?" I asked the nigga Vin.

"I ain't saying shit. I guess y'all going to just have to be mad, huh?" He uttered.

"If I was you, I would talk soon. You might bleed out." I thought I was hearing shit until I turned around and Miyonna was walking up to us. I looked at her stomach and got mad as hell. I don't know who the fuck called her like she ain't pregnant.

"Fuck you bitch!" He tried to yell at her.

"I am a bitch! That bitch you should have never fucked with." Miyonna told him. "Now who the fuck paid you to shoot me?" She must have been listening to us talk. He wasn't saying anything still.

"Fuck it! We just going to kill his ass. Nobody about to play with his ass." I told them. All you heard was click clack around the room.

"Before you die, did your boss send you to kill me?" Miyonna asked him.

"Nope. It wasn't him." He barely got out. I could see that he was losing consciousness from all the blood that was running out.

"Cool." Guns were lifted and just as we were about to pull the trigger, this nigga Vin yelled out something that had me shocked. I made sure to empty my entire clip in his ass. His body jerked as all that lead went through. Nigga looked like he was popping his body. I was glad I had the damn garbage bag on.

"Clean this shit up niggas. Miyonna, let's go!" I grabbed her hand and pulled her along. I made sure to trash the garbage bag along the way. When we got to my car, I pushed her lightly inside.

"I drove here." She tried to protest.

"I don't care. Get your ass in the fucking car!" I yelled at her. "One of your girls can drive your car home."

"Fine." She crossed her arms like I was fazed." When I saw Drea and the girls walking out, I waved them over.

"Here." I handed her Miyonna's keys. "Drive her car home for me." I rolled the window up and started the car up to pull off.

We drove in silence at first.

"Juelz, you think what he said was true?" Miyonna asked. When we stopped at the red light, I looked at her. She had tears in her eyes.

"I don't know, Mimi."

"I want to go and see. I need to talk to her." Miyonna said, but I ignored her. "I'm not going to be able to relax if I don't see about it. This shit is crazy."

"Alright, Mimi. I will take you tomorrow, and we can find out. Okay?" I asked her, and she nodded.

"Since you in the talking mood, who told you where we were? And what made you get your ass out of bed? You supposed to be on bedrest?"

"Dun called me like I asked him to. Shit, I was the one that was shot!"

"So, fuck the baby and your health?" I looked at her, as we pulled up to the house.

"I didn't say that. At the same time, why are you yelling at me when you didn't give a fuck about the baby when you were pushing and choking on me." She got out the car and slammed the door. She walked inside, and I pulled off. I had to handle this shit. Pulling up to my destination, I got out and rang the doorbell. As soon as it opened, I hit dude with a quick right hand. He swung back and caught me in the face. I was ready to fuck shit up for real now. Swinging again, I got him in the nose.

"Oh my gosh! Stop!" I heard a female yell out. I looked and didn't know the girl.

"Mya back up!" Dun told her as he held his nose.

"No. Who is this, and why are you fighting him?" She asked him.

"Mind your business, bitch!" I told her.

"Chill. Don't talk to her like that! What the fuck are you doing here? The fuck you wanna fight for?"

"Why the fuck you tell Mimi what was going on? She pregnant and was put on bedrest. The fuck was flowing through your mind?"

"She asked me to tell her shit when I found out, so I did. Now, get the fuck out!"

"I think you want to fuck my wife. Fall the fuck back." I let him know.

"If I wanted to fuck her, I could have. Especially way before you even came into the picture. Get the fuck out my house!"

"I'm going, but fall the fuck back, or next I come over here, I'm shooting first."

"I bust guns, too, nigga! Ain't no bitch nigga shit over here, my dude." He said back to me. We were just staring at each other.

"You heard what I said." I walked out the door. I knew that nigga wasn't a bitch, but I didn't care. That wasn't smart for him to call Miyonna. She needs to focus on the damn pregnancy and her health. Nothing else mattered at that point.

I hopped in my car and headed home, but I took the long way so that I could clear my head. It was one eventful as night. I still couldn't wrap my mind around what that nigga Vin said before we offed him. At the same time, it does kind of look like it, because of the way shit was happening. I was ready to start some surveillance shit. We had to know the truth.

When I pulled up to the house, I saw that Miyonna's car was in the driveway. I walked in and saw that Janetta was there. She must have been back from her small vacation. She was making her way up the stairs, and I was right behind her. I checked on the boys, and they were knocked out, so I went and checked on Mimi. I walked in, and she was sitting up in the bed.

"Where did you go?" She asked.

"To handle something. Why are you still up?"

"Mya called me. Why did you go over there acting a damn fool? Be mad at me. There was no need for all that." She tried snapping at me.

"You really going to defend that nigga, huh?" I asked in disbelief.

"You were wrong."

"Yo, goodnight! I hope you find my wife, cuz I don't know who you are. You really tripping. I walked out the room and headed to the room that I was sleeping in. I took a shower then hopped on the bed and drifted to a peaceful ass sleep.

Waking up the next morning, I was on a mission. I hurried and handled my hygiene so I could be out. Dressing in all black, I was ready to go. I old Janetta that I was leaving, then I was out the door.

I rode to my destination and parked. I had a clear view of everything, especially when my target walked out the door. They looked around before hopping in the car and pulling out the driveway. I made sure to stay two cars behind them on the road. We rode for a while until we stopped in front of a restaurant, then I parked a few cars down from them. I waited for them to get near the door before I got out and followed. I walked in and was greeted by someone.

"Table for one?" She asked, and I looked around until I found my target.

"Sorry. Yes. Table for one. Can you give the one over there in the far back?"

"Yes. Follow me, sir." The lady walked ahead, and I walked behind her with my hat pulled down low. Making sure my eyes were covered. Where my seat was, I had a perfect view of my target. "Can I start you with something to drink?"

"Yes. Can I just have a glass of orange juice for now?"

"Coming up."

"Thank you." I told her then watched the target. I pulled my phone out to act like I was on it, but I was really taking pictures. Mont wasn't going to believe this shit. I made sure to zoom in. When I was done, I sent the pictures to him. I continued to watch as the waitress walked back to the table.

"You ready to order?" She asked after she sat the glass of juice down.

"Yes. Can I get the Hearty Man Platter? I want my eggs sunny side up."

"Is that it?"

"Can I have toast on the side, too. That's all. Thank you."

"You're welcome." I told her as my phone vibrated in my hand.

Mont: that's really her, my nigga?

Me: yup! That's her grimy ass.

Mont: I wanna put my foot up her ass.

Me: I feel you. I took pictures so that she can't deny it at all.

Mont: word. We going to meet up?

Me: yes. About an hour.

Mont: word. I'm getting dressed now.

Me: see ya in a minute.

Slipping my phone into my pocket, I slowly drank my orange juice as I watched. I was so caught up in trying to read lips that I didn't even realize that my food was sat there on the table. I looked up when I heard the waitress walking away. I turned my focus back to what I was watching, but I broke my stare just to eat my food. I made sure to watch out the corner of eyes. I was almost finished when I saw my target get up and head towards the exit. I waited a few minutes, then I stood up and dropped two hundred dollars on the table before heading towards the exit.

I stood at the entrance as I saw them get in their car. I waited until they were inside before I quickly stepped to my own car. I hopped in and hurried to follow them. All I could do was shake my head as all these thoughts rushed through my head.

When we pulled back up to the house, I sat outside and watched to see if they were going to leave out again. I waited for about three hours, and there was no movement so I decided to get out. I was going in to see if they would act weird in my presence. After getting out, I walked to the door slowly before ringing the doorbell. It took them a minute before someone answered and when they did, I was greeted with a smile.

Chapter 16: Tiyonna Pierce

I was in my room on the phone when I heard someone at the door. I was about to answer it, but was too late, because my mom made it to the door before me, so I started back to my room. I was almost there when I heard a familiar voice, so I stood there and listened. I could tell that my mom was nervous as hell by the tone of her voice. After lying and saying that she didn't feel good, the person left. For some reason, I still stood there and listened to my mother, and she called someone on the phone. She sounded like she was panicked.

"Lu, I think her husband is on to us. He just showed up unexpectedly! What the fuck am I supposed to do?" She started to sound like she was about to cry. She was quiet for a while. I guess he was saying something to her that I couldn't hear. I continued to stand there, though. I wanted to see what my mom was up to that was causing her to act so weirdly. She said a few okays and uhm-hmms before she spoke again.

"Of course, I love you. You shouldn't even question that at all, but at the same time, I arranged for my daughter to be shot. I wanted her to really suffer for being so rude to me."

My mouth dropped. Who the fuck did my mother think she was to sit there and try to have someone kill my sister? Of course I get on Miyonna's nerves, but that just be me being the little sister. I love my sister and brother more than anything, though. I hurried and quick-stepped back to my mom where I texted Owen so that he could come and pick me up. The day he turned eighteen, he moved out. He didn't say nothing to my mom, either. He and his girlfriend pulled up to the house and took all his shit then left. He always says I do too much, but what he did was very extreme. Anyways, I don't see him much, but I still texted him every day to make sure he was okay.

Me: OWEN! ITS AN EMERGENCY. COME AND PICK ME UP!

Owen: What's wrong? I'm on my way.

Me: mommy on some shit. I'll tell you when you get here.

Owen: okay. We will be there in like ten minutes.

I laid my phone on the bed as I packed a small duffle bag up then threw some clothes on. I slipped my black Jordan's on my feet and threw my hair up in a bun after putting my Black Lives Matter hoodie on. Just as I was unplugging my charger to put it in my purse, Owen texted me that he was outside, so I grabbed my stuff up and headed out the door. I saw that Owen was with his girlfriend, which made me roll my eyes. It wasn't that I didn't like her; I just felt like this wasn't her business at all.

"What you rolling your eyes for?" Owen asked when I slid in the back seat.

"No offense, Yanni, but I don't know why he brought you with him. This is sort of family business."

"Shut your ass up, Tiyonna. She my girl so she is family. Now, what's going on with mommy?"

"She did some foolery! She…"

"Man, Tiyonna I'm not about to play with you. Stop beating around the bush and shit. I'mma drop your ass off."

"Shut up, Owen! Drive to Mimi's house. It involves her, too." I sighed deeply. "Mommy set Mimi up to be shot!" I said, and then Owen slammed on the breaks. He looked back at me and so did Yanni.

"How you know that? Who told you that?" He was rambling.

"I heard her talking on the phone. Juelz did a pull-up, and she was acting all nervous and shit, so then she told him that she felt sick. He left, then she got on the phone and called someone." I told him everything, and when I was done, he was sitting there looking shocked.

"Damn! Fuck man!" He banged on the steering wheel before pulling off. "I knew her ass was up to something, but I didn't know what it was. When we visited Mimi, you saw how strange and uninterested she was acting. Stupid bitch!"

"I knew Mommy was mad at Mimi for how she chose to live, but to do all this was unnecessary." I threw out there.

"For real! With her hating ass!" Was all he said as he drove.

I laid my head back on the seat and tried to block out all the noise and war that was about to go down after we told Mimi and Juelz what was up. I kind of want to wait to tell her since she was pregnant, but at the same time, I didn't want to withhold anything from her. Damned if I, and damned if I don't was how I was feeling.

It felt like we were riding forever before we finally got to Mimi's house. We pulled in the driveway, and I saw that it was more than just Mimi and Juelz's cars there. We all got out and rang the doorbell. Ameerah came and opened the door.

"Hey y'all!" She said, and I walked around her. Nobody had time for the small talk. "That was rude, Tiyonna!" Ameerah told me when they walked in.

"You was in the way, and I have something important to tell my sister." I turned back around and saw that Mimi was sitting on one couch with Juelz, and Mont was on the other couch.

"What you have to tell me?" Mimi asked, as she looked from me to Owen then back to me.

"I'm glad you sitting down, because this crazy."

"Always dragging something. Spit it out."

"Okay. Mommy was the one responsible for you getting shot. She paid someone to do it and was kind of pissed that you ain't handicap." I told her, and she looked shocked and so did Ameerah, but Mont and Juelz didn't.

"You sure, Tiyonna?" She asked me, and I nodded my head before explaining everything to her. She all of a sudden got mad as hell and started going off. I guess her getting that excited made her water break, cuz next thing I knew, I heard yelling.

Andrea

"OH MY GOD! IT'S TIME FOR BABY GIRL TO COME!" She sounded so spoiled and extra at the moment, but I let her have it.

"Come on. You can go and change then we can go to the hospital." Juelz told her, and I was a little worried that it might be too soon for her to have the baby. They headed up the stairs just as the boys were coming down with Princess. They saw me and got excited.

"TiTi! When did you get here?" They asked.

"A little while ago. What was y'all doing?"

"In the playroom. Princess spilled juice so we came down here." Mahki said, as he gave her the evil eye. He must have been mad, because usually he loved him some Princess.

"Okay. Let's go clean it." I grabbed their hands, and we headed back up the stairs after I stopped in the kitchen for some napkins. We cleaned the floor and then they went back to playing. I sat in the room with them for a while until Janetta came in. That was when I left and headed back downstairs just in time to see that everyone was leaving. I was going to the hospital, too. As soon as we were pulling in front of the hospital, my phone rang. I looked and saw that it was my mom calling. I rolled my eyes before answering.

"Yes, Ma?"

"Where are you? I didn't even know that you left. What's going on?"

"I'm with Owen at the hospital…" I started to say, but she cut me off.

"Oh my gosh! Is my baby okay?"

"Yeah. He fine. We here, cuz Mimi water broke. She in labor."

"Hmm. Oh." She said it so dry.

"Why you say it like that, Ma? There is no need for you to be acting like that at all. At the end of the day, Mimi is still your daughter. You acting stupid for no reason." I told her then hung up. I looked up, and Owen was staring at me.

"Who was that?"

"Mommy."

"Hmm." He shook his head.

Chapter 17: Miyonna Pierce- Johnson

I couldn't believe that the shit my sister told me sent my ass into labor. I was mad, but at the same time, it bought me some time to plan out what I was going to do to my mother. She had me fucked up if she thought that I was about to let that she got someone to shoot me go. Then, she wanted me paralyzed and shit. I didn't think so. I wanted her to think that everything was all good, but after I have this baby and my six weeks check-up, I was on that ass! I promise I was.

As I rode to the hospital, all I could think about was getting the baby out of me. This might be my most intense labor I have had, and I was not feeling it at all. I was so glad when we pulled up to the hospital. Juelz helped me out the car and carried me in. When he told them that I was in labor, they hurried and brought me a wheelchair. After I was seated, I was wheeled off and taken straight to Labor and Delivery. I was glad that I dilated quickly and was ready to push.

As I was getting ready to push, something wasn't right at all. I had the worst feeling, and I wasn't just talking about the feeling that I had from the labor. My other feeling was more of something is going to happen that was bad.

"Push, Mrs. Johnson! Push down as hard as you can." Dr. Lee told me, and I did what I was told.

"Ahhhhhhhhhhhhh!" I yelled as I pushed.

"Keep going. You are crowning. I see the head." The doctor told me.

"Come on, bae. You can do this! It's all going to be worth it when she is here." Juelz called himself coaching me.

"Oh my gosh! Shut up, Juelz, and get away from me. It's all your fault!" I snapped at him. I was sweating hard as hell. My hair curled back to its natural state after I had straightened it out.

"Push, bae." He wiped my forehead, and I swear the cool rag felt so good against it.

"Shit! Ahhhhhhhhhhhhhhhhhhhhh!" I pushed down extra hard, and I felt her coming out.

"Here she is!" I heard the doctor say, but I didn't hear the baby crying at all. Juelz walked over to them.

"Why is she so quiet?" I asked, and no one said anything, which made me yell out and ask them again. Juelz walked back over to me.

"Calm down. He is suctioning her. She probably couldn't breathe for a second. Relax, please!" He told me, then kissed me on the forehead, but I ignored him and focused on the baby still not crying.

"Something is wrong, and you are trying to distract me."

"The baby isn't breathing." The doctor finally said.

"Oh my god!" I went off, and the last thing I heard was the doctor saying that they were going to sedate me. Next thing I know, I was out!

Andrea

Waking up, I looked around and saw that I wasn't in the delivery room anymore. I was somewhere else, but I was still in the hospital. I looked around and saw Juelz sleep on a chair. I wondered where my sister and brother were, though. Ameerah and Mont, too.

"Juelz!" I called out to him.

"Oh, shit. You up?"

"I only been sleep a few hours." I told him.

"More like two days." He said, and I looked at him.

"Where is the baby? Did she die? I remember that she wasn't breathing."

"The baby is fine. She in the NICU." He walked over to me, then leaned down and kissed me on the lips. That was the most affectionate that we had been in so long. "She look like me." He smiled.

"I want to see her."

"Let me buzz the doctor to let them know that you are up." I watched as he hit the button, and a few minutes later, a few nurses come up.

"You're up, Mrs. Johnson. Let's check your vitals."

"I want to see my baby."

"You can after we check your vitals. We will get you a wheelchair and wheel you down to see her."

"Okay."

I laid still and let her do what she had to do. When she finally was finished with what she was doing, she helped me in the wheelchair and took me to the NICU. When we got there,

I looked at the few babies. That instantly made me emotional, but I got it together. I was excited when they stopped me in front of my baby girl. She looked so much like Juelz. You could tell that we didn't get along during my pregnancy. I waited for the nurse to come and help with the baby. She took her out the incubator and gently laid her in my arms.

Miracle Jai'Yona is the prettiest little baby I had ever seen. She was looking like the female version of Juelz, just a lot softer. The nurse brought me a bottle so that I could feed her, and I had tears in my eyes again as I began. I didn't like the fact that she was in the NICU. I was going to wait until I was done feeding her to talk to the nurse and doctor to see what caused the baby to not be breathing when she came out.

Almost a half-hour later, I was done feeding the baby, and the nurse walked back in. After she put the baby back in the incubator, I told her that I wanted to talk to her and the doctor. They wheeled me back into my room while Juelz stayed with baby girl. I didn't mind, though. He probably had already talked to the doctor.

"What did you want to talk to us about?" The doctor asked, when he walked in the room, and I was situated back in bed.

"Can you tell me why the baby wasn't breathing when she came out?" I got straight to the point.

"There was a lot of fluid that we drained from her lungs. That was a key factor. The chord was another thing, but it wasn't wrapped tightly around her neck. We removed her in time."

"Thank you. How much did she weigh?" I asked.

"Four pounds and six ounces. She is sixteen inches long. That's another reason why she is in the NICU. We need her to gain some more weight before we can release her."

"Okay. That's understandable. Thank you so much."

"You're welcome. Do you want to go back down to see her?"

"No. Not right now. My husband can enjoy some alone time with her." I told them, and they nodded before walking out. I was worried about my baby, but at the same time, I wasn't, because I knew that they would make sure she is okay.

As the thoughts of my daughter ran through my mind, so did those of my mother. I couldn't believe her ass. I had something nice planned for her ass, though. All I had to do was send Drea and her girls a text. I knew that they would do exactly what I wanted them to. They always came through for me; that was why I didn't mind them working for me as well as doing their own thing.

I decided to try and get some rest. I felt slightly sluggish and emotional so I thought it would be best to take a nap. Just as I closed my eyes, I heard someone walk in. I felt their presence strong, but they didn't say anything. I opened my eyes and saw that it was my mother. She looked at me, and I smiled at her. I didn't want her to think anything ill at the moment.

214

"Congratulations, Miyonna. I hope you teach her to be a lady and not a wannabe thug." *There her ass goes taking shots at me.*

"Thank you, and I sure will, because I don't know nothing about being a wannabe thug. Can't teach what I don't know." I matched her tone.

"Here you go." She sat a gift bag down. I grabbed it and looked inside. There was a receiving blanket and some booties in there. I stared at the gift then chuckled.

"Thanks."

"You're welcome. So where is the baby?"

"In the NICU. Juelz is down there with her."

"Why is she in there?" She asked like she was concerned.

"She wasn't breathing when she came out, and she is early."

"How did you go in labor?"

"Got some crazy ass news. It took me over the edge, and my water broke." I smirked.

"Damn. You know better than to be getting worked up like that."

"You're right, but this news was nuts. It was inevitable. Anyway, who told you that I went into labor?"

"Tiyonna. She actually told me yesterday. I came to see you last night, but you were knocked out."

"Yeah." Was all I said.

"Okay. Well, I will see you later."

Andrea

"Alright. Bye." I waved at her. She walked out as Juelz was walking in. I handed him the gift bag and watched him look through it. He had the same reaction as me.

"She was serious?"

"Dead ass!" He tossed the whole bag in the trash. I ain't care, though. I needed to rest for real.

. . .

Six weeks had passed, and we were home. The baby came home about two weeks after I did. I was happy because she gained two pounds which made her big enough to leave the hospital. Baby girl greedy as hell, but I loved it. She was about to be a thick 'ems like her mom.

Anyways, my six-week was up, and I was on a mission. Drea had already called me and let me know that she did what I asked her to, so now, I was on my way to meet Dun at the spot. I was dressed in all black and ready for whatever. I ended up pulling up the same time as Dun.

"You ready to do this?" He asked.

"Yes I am." I answered, and we walked in the door. We walked in, and my mother as well as her boyfriend Luther was tied to a chair. They had tape across their mouths. I stood in front of them and noticed that they were out of it. "I told y'all not to kill them."

"We didn't. Watch this!" Drea walked over and grabbed two jars of what looked like to be piss and tossed it on both of them, and their eyes popped open. I stepped back, because once I smelled it, I realized that it was cat piss, which was strong as hell.

"Hey, Ma and Stepdad." I smirked.

"What are you doing, Miyonna?"

"Sending you where you sent my dad and tried to send me. You know I was going to let you rock and just not ever speak to you or have my kids around you ever again until I found out that you were responsible for my dad's death. I don't know who you thought you were. Payback is a bitch. Then, you had the nerve to be working with someone who hated my father and my father hated him. You were dead ass serious. All I want to know is why. I mean, you fucking someone who does the same thing as my dad."

"Your dad was a part of a set-up. Your older brother is actually Luther's son. I got with your father when he was a baby. It was all part of a plan. You don't understand how horrible it was to be with your father and act like I loved him when I really couldn't wait until someone shot his ass up! Then, when he died, he had a nerve to pass it down to you, which made you my man's biggest competition, and you actually loved what you were doing. You had to face the same fate. I hate that you didn't die. All you had to do was decline it. Luther would have taken over all the customers and was even willing to take in you, your sister, and brother. You disrespected him by taking the position and disrespect is not allowed." She had the nerve to say. I fell out laughing causing everyone to laugh.

Andrea

"Yall can laugh now, but even if you kill us, we will have the last laugh from the afterlife. My people will kill you all." Luther said and really had us going.

"I doubt it. All your men are dead. I made sure my girls took them all out before kidnapping you and my mother. Y'all are the last to go. It's only right to save the best for last, right?" I chuckled.

"Fuck you!"

"No thanks! You can fuck my mother more in the afterlife when y'all get there. Now, I don't want to hold this up anymore. I'mma make this shit simple. Anything you want to say before you go?"

"God don't like ugly and you reap what you sew." My mother said, and I shook my head.

"Ain't that the pot calling the kettle black! I'mma make sure to get custody of my sister, though. I'mma always take care of her. It's crazy that she was the one that came and told me that your ass had me shot. I hope you get a mansion in hell with Luther. Wait, first you can sign these papers." I pulled them out of my hoodie pocket before shoving them in her face. She saw how serious I was and signed them. When she was done, I stuffed them back in my pocket before I lifted my gun up. I looked at Dun, and he did the same thing. We emptied the clip in both of them. I knew that they were dead, but that wasn't enough for me.

"Drag them out to the back for me!" I asked the men that were there. I walked away, grabbed a gas can, and told one of

218

the dudes to spark a blunt. Once we were in the back, they smoked some of the blunt while I doused my mother and Luther's body with some gas. I grabbed the blunt and dropped it on them. We sat and watched as their bodies burned. The smell of burnt flesh was strong as hell. I heard someone gagging behind me, but I shut them out. I had so much satisfaction watching them burn up.

"Anybody want to roll them up and smoke them?" I joked, but everyone declined anyway. I grabbed a bucket of water and poured it all over the ashes. It was like they were never there. I didn't care, though. "Clean the building up. Make sure everyone is at my house tomorrow morning. I have an announcement to make. It's important, too." I told them as I headed for the door. I hopped in my car and headed home.

Pulling up to my house, I got this happy and exciting feeling. I felt like everything was falling back into place with Juelz, and I was glad for that, but I knew that it would fully be in place by the morning.

Walking inside, I saw that the boys were in the living room with Janetta watching a movie. It was past their bedtime, but I didn't even push. I just headed upstairs to my bedroom. I walked in and had to fan myself because Juelz was laid across the bed in some shorts and no shirt on with Jai'Yona laid against his chest. She was curled up knocked out, and he was channel surfing. I started to strip and headed to the bathroom. I didn't want to go near them dirty. After taking a quick shower, I put on some pajama pants and a tank top then climbed in bed. I knew my legs were going to be dry and ashy in the morning, but I didn't even care. I just wanted to be under my man.

"Everything good?" Juelz asked.

"Yeah it is now. Thank you for letting me handle it on my own."

"You're welcome. I know that you needed that closure." He said, and I leaned over and kissed him. "What was that for?"

"For being the best husband any girl could ask for. I know our relationship been crazy these last few months, but I'm thankful and glad that you didn't give up on me. On us. Just know that I love you and our kids more than anything in the world."

"I love you, too. Don't ever question it. This is till death do us part. We got too much invested in this commitment. Just know that, when I left, it was cuz I was so close to putting my hands on you for real. I never want to have that feeling again. Some shit has to change."

"I know. You will see just how much in the morning. It's going to be an epic surprise. Trust me!" I smiled at him, and he looked at me with raised eyebrow, but I didn't say anything. I gently took the baby from him and laid her in the bassinet that was next to the bed. After putting the blanket across her, I climbed back in the bed. I saw that Juelz was texting on his phone.

"I'm texting Janetta downstairs to let her know that, after the movie was over, the boys need to go to bed." He said, before I could ask him who he was texting.

"Oh. Shit, I meant to check on my sister." I got up. My sister had been staying at my house since the day that I went to the hospital and gave birth. I walked down to her room and knocked on the bed before walking in. I laughed at her laid across the bed texting away on her phone with earphones in her ears. I tapped her foot getting her attention.

"Oh, hey Mimi." She sat up.

"You good?"

"Yeah. I'm cool."

"Okay. You sure?" I asked her, and she nodded. "Here is the story. Mommy signed over her rights and gave you the papers before telling you to get out. Then, you haven't seen her since."

"Okay. You know that you have to go to a meeting at my school since Mommy was supposed to go."

"Alright. Just remind me about it." I told her.

"Okay." She nodded.

"Kay. Goodnight." I stood up.

"I hope I don't hear y'all in there hunching."

"You got earphones. You will be okay, girl." I laughed, as I walked out the door closing it behind me. I walked back down to my room. I was so exhausted and ready to fall into a deep sleep. I climbed into the bed once more and got comfortable under Juelz. I laid my head on his chest and was so comfortable. I started to doze off when I felt Juelz run his hands up and down my thighs. I tried to ignore him, but he slipped a hand into my shorts and rubbed on my pussy making me wet. I turned and looked up at him. I saw it in his eyes that he wanted some so I was about to have one hell of a night with one hell of a husband.

Chapter 18: Juelz Johnson

Waking up this morning, I knew that it was going to be a good morning. That's just the way I woke up. I looked over at Mimi's naked body, and all I could think about was the way she rode my dick. All night long until she came hard as hell then I flipped her over on her hands and knees and sent her ass over the edge knocking her ass right to sleep. I blew out a whistle just thinking about it as I headed into the bathroom to handle my hygiene. I took a quick shower before walking out with my towel wrapped around me, and I saw that Mimi was up with the baby now. She looked up at me and smiled.

"Morning." I told her, and she said it back. "Let me throw some clothes on then I'll take her while you go get in the shower and whatever."

"Okay. Everyone should be here by noon for brunch, so I'm about to go and start cooking the food." She called out to me. I threw on some gray joggers and a white t-shirt. It wasn't like I planned on going out today. I was spending it inside.

"That's cool." I called back to her.

I walked out the closet with my slippers on. I walked over and took the baby out her arms. I watched as she climbed out the bed. Her body was perfect to me. She had a little stomach from the baby, but I didn't mind it. My wife was still beautiful and fly.

I walked out the room with Miracle in my arms, and I walked to the boys' room. I was surprised that they were still sleeping. Any other time, they would be on the game. I guess they were tired from their movie night. I woke them up and told them to go and wash their faces and brush their teeth while I found them something to wear. I walked into their closet and found them some sweats and a shirt each. I laid each of their clothes on their bed. Then, I grabbed them some boxers and socks laying them down too.

"Get in the shower. Jr, go first. Then, watch Mahki when he gets in. Make sure to adjust the water for him."

"Okay." Jr told me, and I walked out their room. I walked back to my bedroom to see if Mimi was dressed so that she could bathe baby girl. I wanted to wake and bake. Lucky for me, she was walking out with her bra and panties on.

"Bae, get her dressed. I'm 'bout to go down to the basement."

"Lay her in her bassinet while I throw something on." She said, and I did. Then, I walked out the room bumping right into Tiyonna.

"My sister up?"

"Yeah. She in there getting dressed."

I told her then jogged down the stairs. I walked into my cave and plopped on the couch. I grabbed my weed and rolled up while I turned the morning news on. As I watched, I couldn't help but think about what Mimi's surprise was that she had for me. I lit my blunt and let the weed flow through my veins. I faced the whole thing, and now I was ready for a whole good meal. I was in the basement for a while, so I knew that Mimi had to be downstairs and had started to cook. I walked up the stairs and opened the door, and the smell of food smacked me right in the face. I followed the smell and saw that Tiyonna and Mimi were cooking while baby girl sat in her bouncer. I went by baby girl while I watched Mimi move around the kitchen.

...

It was a little after eleven when I heard the doorbell ring. I checked to see who it was and saw that it was Mont, Princess, and Ameerah. I opened the door and dapped my boy up before hugging Meerah and Princess. Of course, Meerah headed to the kitchen and Princess ran up the stairs to the boys' room. Me and my boy just kicked it in the living room. By noon, the house was full as hell, and everyone was in the living room. We were waiting for Mimi to come and say what she had to say.

"I know that I said that I had something to say so here it is." Mimi said, then sighed with a smiled. "Okay, with everything that has happened since I was shot and all that good shit, I decided to step down some. I'm not fully quitting. Just fading to the back and letting Dun handle everything. Too much has happened, and it almost cost me my marriage and family. Lord knows that they are the most important things in my life, and I need to remember that so I am going to focus more on them. So, with that being said, Janetta, we won't need you as much. I mean, of course we are going to need you to babysit from time to time, but that's about it. Thank you for everything." Mimi said, and I was shocked. Her ass was stepping down! She moved closer to me and hugged me tightly before kissing me on the lips. I was tearing her pussy down to the mattress later on. "Okay. Mont has an announcement to make." She said, and we all looked at him.

"Damn! Y'all staring hard as hell at a nigga." He joked, and we all laughed. He looked at Ameerah and smirked at her. "So Ameerah, I heard you was talking slick 'bout a nigga, and how you were about to leave me, cuz we been together for years, and you still don't have a ring. Well, you know I like to move at my own pace, but at the same time, I want to apologize, cuz you work my nerves and make me want to strangle you one minute, then fuck you the next, but hey, that's just us, and I love your bipolar ass. You know I ain't a mushy ass nigga and shit, but you wanna marry me? I mean, either way, you stuck with a nigga forever, so you might as well just say yes." He told her and tears welled up in her eyes as we all laughed quickly before stopping and waiting for her to answer.

"Yes!" She answered, excitedly.

"I already knew it. Come here." He pulled her close to him and slipped the ring on her finger. She looked down at it then back up at him.

"Well, since everyone making announcements." Ameerah started saying then smiled before continuing. "I'm pregnant!" She said.

"Awe, shit! A nigga bout to be a dad again!" Mont was hyped.

"I'mma be a god mom again." Mimi had to chime in.

"Yup to both of y'all. Now, let's eat! Stomach growling and stuff!" Ameerah said, and we headed to the dining room.

The End for Miyonna and Juelz.

Stay tuned for part two with Drea and her crew as well as Ameerah and Mont's wedding. You think we had drama. Get ready for the ride that Drea and them bout to take you on. You not even ready.

Don't forget to leave your girl a review. Good or bad.

CPSIA information can be obtained
at www.ICGtesting.com
Printed in the USA
LVOW10s1330300817
546968LV00022BA/564/P